# VOYAGERS
## THE THIRD GHOST

**An Insecure Writer's Support Group Anthology**

FREEDOM FOX PRESS
Dancing Lemur Press, L.L.C.
Pikeville, North Carolina
www.dancinglemurpress.com

Copyright 2020 by The Insecure Writer's Support Group
Published by Freedom Fox Press
An imprint of:
Dancing Lemur Press, L.L.C., P.O. Box 383, Pikeville, North Carolina,
27863-0383
www.dancinglemurpress.com

ISBN: 9781939844729

This book is a work of fiction. Any resemblance to actual events or
persons, living or dead, is coincidental.

Cover design by C.R.W.

Library of Congress Cataloging-in-Publication Data
Names: Insecure Writer's Support Group, compiler.
Title: Voyagers : the third ghost : an Insecure Writers Support Group
    anthology.
Description: Pikeville, North Carolina : Freedom Fox Press, Dancing
Lemur
    Press, L.L.C., [2020] | Includes bibliographical references. |
Audience:
    Ages 8-14. | Summary: "Journey into the past... Will the third ghost
be
    found before fires take more lives? Can everyone be warned before
    Pompeii is buried again? What happens if a blizzard traps a family
in
    East Germany? Will the Firebird help Soviet sisters outwit evil
during
    WWII? And sneaking off to see the first aeroplane - what could go
    wrong?"-- Provided by publisher.
Identifiers: LCCN 2019060026 (print) | LCCN 2019060027 (ebook) |
ISBN
    9781939844729 (paperback) | ISBN 9781939844736 (ebook)
Subjects: LCSH: Short stories, American. | Historical fiction. | Short
    stories. | CYAC: Short stories. | History--Fiction. | Adventure and
    adventurers--Fiction.
Classification: LCC PZ5 .M367 2019 (print) | LCC PZ5 (ebook) |
DDC
    [Fic]--dc23
LC record available at https://lccn.loc.gov/2019060026
LC ebook record available at https://lccn.loc.gov/2019060027

The Insecure Writer's Support Group would like to thank the judges who selected the stories for this anthology. We appreciate their time and effort!

**Elizabeth S. Craig -** Cozy mystery author for Penguin Random House, Midnight Ink, and independently.

**Dianne K. Salerni** - author of the The Eighth Day fantasy series and historical novels, The Caged Graves and We Hear the Dead.

**S.A. Larsen** - international award-winning author of the middle grade fantasy-adventure Motley Education and the young adult contemporary-fantasy romance Marked Beauty.

**Lindsay Davis Auld** - As an agent, she is eager to help bring fresh voices, characters and stories to a new generation of readers.

**Rachna Chhabria** - author of numerous children's books and a columnist with Deccan Chronicle and The Asian Age.

**Lynda Dietz** - a copyeditor who works with authors in a variety of genres, both in fiction and nonfiction.

**Tonja Drecker** – author of Music Boxes, blogger, children's book reviewer, and freelance translator.

**David Powers King** – author of Woven, The Undead Road, and Full Dark: An Anthology.

# Table of Contents

# The Third Ghost
## By Yvonne Ventresca

*Hoboken, New Jersey*
*October 1981*

**L**ewis checked on his little sister before he snuck out in the middle of the night. Christina slept peacefully, clutching the most recent book they'd been reading together. Despite the fact they were still several sizes too big, she wore his old Bugs Bunny pjs again. As he tucked the blanket around her, a weird sense of foreboding overcame him, as if he should wake her and say goodbye one last time. But that was ridiculous. Nothing had ever happened the other times he slipped away. He would be home soon enough.

Usually, he took the stairwell from their second-floor apartment and crept out the back door. The wooden steps often creaked, but he'd mastered the art of moving quietly and slinking along undetected. But tonight, just as Lewis cracked the door to leave the apartment, his neighbor stumbled down the hall toward him. The man always asked too many questions in his booming voice. Luckily, he stopped a moment to light a cigarette with unsteady hands. When the flame of the lighter flickered, Lewis used the distraction to jerk the door closed, cringing at the click that seemed magnified in the night.

*That was close.*

Plan B: the back window. He returned to the rear bedroom. Moving slowly, he pushed the screenless window open. His sister stirred, fluttered her eyes a moment, but went back to sleep without noticing him.

He stared at the ground below, strewn with broken glass and garbage. *I've done this before.* He put his right leg over the sill. *No broken bones yet.*

As he climbed out, he hung from the window ledge, shortening the distance of his drop. Mom had told them about the hanging technique, instead of jumping, in case they needed to escape in an emergency. All the parents worried about fire after the recent arson deaths.

Letting go was the scariest part. He waited as long as possible, until he could barely hold on, then released his grip. He landed on his feet with an *oomph*, falling forward from the impact. As he wiped his palms on his jeans, he checked his hands for cuts. Nothing bad.

An eerie darkness blanketed the rear of the building. Clouds blocked the moon, and the October wind whirled the dead leaves across the ground. Something metal clanked nearby, and Lewis startled at the sound.

*Stay asleep, Christina.* She'd always been a sound sleeper, and he counted on that now. He didn't want her waking up afraid, wondering about the window and his absence.

Even though that hadn't ever happened, he hesitated. He was debating if he should go back inside when male voices rumbled nearby. He peered around the edge of the building. Two men who were deep in discussion didn't acknowledge his fall. Thank goodness.

Saturday nights were always the trickiest for him, when too many people stayed out late. Before the men noticed him, he hurried away, adrenaline fueling his fast stride. Not that he was doing anything technically wrong. There was no legal reason an almost-thirteen-year-old couldn't be outside in the middle of the night, right?

He shivered. Maybe it was because of the men huddled in the dark. Or maybe it was because of Halloween next week. Either way, the shadows made him jittery. *I'm not afraid. It's only the wind giving me chills.*

Zipping his jacket, he focused on his mission.

He'd lost track of how many times he felt compelled to execute his new routine. Had it been days or weeks since Mom started working late shifts cleaning at the train station? Since he could never sleep those nights anyway, he would sneak to the Hoboken terminal and quietly follow her home, making sure nothing bad happened to her along the way. She would be furious if she caught him out at night, especially after he'd been sick, so he kept watch from a distance.

Despite some close calls, no one ever stopped him to ask what he was doing out alone. He stayed alert, wary of anyone who might question him. He usually felt safe enough. But tonight, the streetlights cast spooky shapes on the road as the wind howled, low and cold. It reminded him of the book of scary stories he'd taken out of the library over the summer. There had been an especially memorable one about a haunting.

Two cops standing near the Clam Broth House jolted him out of his reverie. He thought for sure they saw him, but he darted behind the next building, pulse pounding in his ears.

"Greed," one of them said. "Pure and simple. The tenements are worth more burned down. The insurance money pays for the renovation."

"They should at least light the fires when no one is home. If the buildings were empty, that would be one thing. But in the middle of the night, people are bound to die. Especially the children."

The second cop grunted in agreement. "No one said arsonists were worried about deadly consequences."

His voice faded as they moved away.

Lewis made himself wait another minute before he left his hiding space. Mom's shift ended at midnight. He was nearly there, with plenty of time to spare. Focused on his destination, he almost tripped over the boy crouched by the corner mailbox. It was as if he'd appeared out of nowhere.

"Whoa!" Lewis dropped his voice to a whisper. "You scared me."

"Sorry." The boy, dressed in sweatpants and a Smurf sweatshirt, was maybe eight or nine, like Christina. "I need help," he said. "Henrietta's stuck. See?" He pointed to a metal pipe under the mailbox. It wasn't attached to anything, as if someone had discarded it. From inside the pipe came a plaintive cry.

Lewis bent to look. Two green eyes blinked at him from inside.

"I need to leave on a voyage," the boy explained, "but I can't go with Henrietta in trouble."

A voyage? The word made Lewis think of ships heading out to sea. The boy didn't look dressed for a boat ride.

"I can't reach her."

"Can you tilt the pipe?" Lewis asked. "Maybe she'll crawl out."

"Too heavy."

Lewis tried to lift it, but it wouldn't budge. A big guy in construction boots hurried past them toward the train station.

"Can you help us?" the boy called, but the man rushed onward, ignoring them.

"Don't worry," Lewis said. "We'll figure something out. What if I push her toward you, then you slide her out?"

The boy nodded.

Lewis tugged the sleeves of his jacket down, not

wanting to get scratched. He checked inside the pipe. All he could see was a ball of black fluff. He gently put his hand on the back of the cat and eased her forward.

A loud meow was followed by a cry of triumph. "Got her!" the boy said, cradling Henrietta until she squirmed. After he placed her on the ground, she meowed again. But on closer inspection, her fur wasn't black. She was a tabby cat covered in soot.

"She doesn't seem hurt or anything," Lewis said as Henrietta sauntered away.

No reply.

When Lewis turned back, the boy had gone. "Hello?" he called. But he stood by himself on the corner.

*Weird. It's almost as if the boy was...No.* The wind blew from the Hudson River and he shuddered. Alone in the night, he did not want to think about ghosts. Shaking off the fear, he continued to the train station.

Still, it reminded him of the story he'd read aloud to Christina, about a kid who had to do something important before he could move on from being a ghost. She hadn't been frightened at all. To calm himself, he imagined telling her about what happened tonight. "And then the boy just disappeared!" The idea of describing the events to his sister got him through the last dark streets, until he safely entered the station.

He was still early, and although he generally stayed out of sight, the idea of being near other people for a few minutes comforted him. He hopped the turnstile without guilt—it wasn't like he was actually taking a ride. Just then an elderly lady hobbled up the stairs. He thought for sure she would scold him, but she seemed preoccupied, so he scurried to the platform. The tracks were empty, but a train would arrive soon enough with disembarking passengers. He imagined boarding one , a way to travel someplace better. A voyage, a grand adventure of his own.

But no. His family needed him. Ten more minutes until Mom finished work. He sat on a bench to wait.

Movement caught his eye. Sometimes, rats scurried along the tracks, but this was a flash of flowing white that contrasted with the darkness of the tunnels. He blinked a few times at the eerie sight. Was it a sheet, something that had blown off the platform? He left the bench to get a better look. As his eyes focused, he froze. A girl walked on the train tracks, her long white nightgown fluttering around her ankles.

Somewhere in the distance, a train rumbled.

"Hey," he called. "Hey!"

She looked at him, questioning.

"Get off the tracks! A train is coming!" Desperate to reach her in time, he rushed toward her as the train rounded the final curve. He leaned over to grab her hand, momentarily transfixed by the approaching headlight. When his hand came up empty, he checked the tracks again. She escaped, but where? Shaken, he stepped away from the edge.

The subway came to a halt with a loud hiss and the doors dinged as they slid open. He turned away and gasped at the sight of the girl, now on the platform. Somehow, she had scrambled to safety in time. She stood apart from the others, as if waiting for someone. He leaned against a pillar to steady his trembling.

The few arriving passengers rushed past them to get home. Soon, they were the only two remaining. She walked onto the train without speaking to him. He stayed, transfixed, and after a few minutes, she came back out.

"You could've gotten killed," he said.

She stared at Lewis, her brown eyes wide with surprise. "I'm fine. I need to go home."

"On the train?"

"No." She motioned toward the stairs. "I live on Clinton Street. I just can't remember the way."

Was she ill, wandering around in her nightgown in a state of confusion? During his feverish state, he'd tried to leave the apartment, thinking he could escape the heat somehow.

"Go straight to the corner," he explained. "Then make your first right by Hotel Victor. Make the next left, and you'll reach Clinton Street."

She smoothed her long black hair off her forehead in a nervous gesture. "It's far."

*Definitely seems ill.* He glanced at the clock. If he walked her home, he could double back and still check on Mom over the last few blocks. This girl wandering around lost was more at risk than his mother.

"I'll come with you, if you want," he said. "It's late to be walking around if you're not sure where you're going."

She nodded, accompanying him to the stairs. She strode with her back straight, eyes forward, no hand on the railing. He shuffled along beside her, sneaking sidelong glances as they left the station. Had she moved here recently? That would explain why she didn't know her way.

"It's kind of creepy out tonight." He looked back at the terminal, hoping Mom would be okay without him watching over her, just this once. "Your family must be worried about you," he said. "What were you doing at the station so late?"

"I wanted to see my father. He works there."

"So does my mom! What does your dad do?"

"He works on the train. I felt like I needed to see him, you know?"

"I do know," he said. It made perfect sense to him, although he didn't run around outside in his pajamas. Still, no one else seemed to pay any attention to her as they traveled along the streets in the darkness. A breeze ruffled her hair as they walked. She didn't look sickly, but something still struck him as odd.

"Do you feel okay?" he asked. "I was really sick over the summer. Throbbing headache, burning fever—"

"No, I'm fine."

At last, they reached Clinton Street.

"I can go from here," she said. "Thank you for keeping me safe on my voyage."

There was that word again, just like the ghostly boy. But before Lewis could respond, she touched his hand, light as air, and that's when the premonition hit him.

He smelled smoke. Not cigarette smoke, but an acrid, burning fire. It only lasted a few seconds, but he turned, searching for the source of the scent. When he looked back, he found empty space. Like the boy before, the girl vanished. He shuddered, not wanting to question how she disappeared or where she went or why this night was so very strange. Did he actually interact with two ghosts?

As bizarre as it seemed, it almost didn't matter. What mattered was the information she had given him, the feeling he knew to be true as he broke into a run.

His building was on fire.

He sensed it in every part of his being, like an anxious ball of heat bouncing inside as he sprinted toward home, to where Christina slept.

From far away, he couldn't see the flames. But the girl had given him the message when she touched him. *Danger. Burning. Fire.* His brain raced as his body ran, and he tried to come up with a rational explanation for what he believed but couldn't possibly know. When he first left home, he heard a clank. Some type of metal fuel can? And the men huddled near his building in the dark. Had they been planning another arson?

He slowed for a moment and considered calling the fire department or the police. But he didn't carry change for a pay phone. He picked up his pace. It felt better to keep going, to get there as soon as he could.

*I will make it in time.* His feet hit the ground in a frantic rhythm that reverberated through him. *I must make it.*

As he covered block after block, he tried to remember anything from the earlier fires that might be helpful. They all burned in the middle of the night. Over twenty people died. The last one—it gutted apartments on Clinton Street.

Of course. Where the girl was from. Could she have been a victim in the fire? And the boy with the soot-covered cat, too? He could barely comprehend what it meant, this night of spirits and dark shadows and howling wind.

*Three blocks to go.*

He thought of his sister sleeping, clutching the book, of all the stories he'd read to her over the years. Things happened in threes. Three little pigs and three granted wishes and...there had only been two ghosts tonight.

The cops he'd overheard said the arsonists should at least start the fires during the day, when the buildings were emptier. Not at night, when sleeping children might die. Children like Christina. He didn't want his sister to join the other ghosts. She couldn't be the third. He forced himself to sprint.

*One block to go.*

If Christina smelled the smoke and woke up, she might have a chance. They weren't that high up. But knowing his sister, she would sleep through it. She slept through everything. And there were no smoke detectors. The landlord had said he would install them, soon, but like many repairs, it hadn't happened yet.

As he turned onto his street, flames erupted from the roof of his building. Even though he expected it, he screamed. The fire was enormous. Sirens wailed in the distance, but he couldn't wait for help. They would never make it to his sister.

He knew what he needed to do, had known it during the whole race home. Using his jacket to shield his face, Lewis burst through the front door of the building, bounding up the stairs two at a time. He yelled to his neighbors as he ran, "Wake up! Fire! You need to get out!"

Thick smoke filled the air as he made his way into their apartment. Reaching the back bedroom, he scooped Christina in his arms.

"Lewis?" She seemed confused, but before she could say more, she coughed, turning her head into his chest to escape the suffocating smoke.

"I've got you." He carried her toward the door.

Too late. The way out was blocked, the entrance engulfed in flames. The bedroom filled with more smoke in the few moments they hesitated.

"We need to use the window." He moved toward the ledge.

She peered out, her small body trembling in his oversized pjs. "I don't know if I can."

Without speaking, he grabbed all the bedding he could and hurled it out the window to cover the broken glass and soften the fall. The heat burned intensely now, reminding him again of his illness— the sweltering inside him and how agonizing it had been, until suddenly the fever stopped.

Somewhere in the building a wooden beam cracked loudly. "We have to leave."

"You first. Show me how."

He wanted her out of danger, but she seemed

frozen in terror. "Okay. But then you need to follow right away. You can't chicken out. Promise?"

"Promise."

He quickly threw his legs over, then dangled from the ledge. "Hang then drop," he told her, right before he let go. Scrambling to his feet, he yelled to her. "Now Christina!" He could barely see her in the smoke. "Now!"

As if in slow motion, one Bugs Bunny-covered leg went over, then another, until his sister hung suspended from the window. He was too short to reach her, and they were running out of time.

"Drop!"

Her hesitation stretched unbearably.

Then Christina reacted. She let go, landing in the center of the pillows and blankets. He quickly rolled her up in case the flames had reached her. But other than the coughing, she seemed all right.

*I did it.*

Keeping her wrapped in a blanket, he carried her farther from the house, away from the heat and embers. The physical exertion caught up with him. Weary, he set Christina down gently.

She blinked, staring at him as if in a dream. "Don't go," she said.

But a college student lived upstairs, and the family with a baby had moved in down the hall. What if other neighbors were trapped? Despite his good intentions, he only made it a few yards before he sank to the ground in front of the burning building, exhausted.

His arm landed awkwardly on a metal container. Fuel? Something the arsonists used to start the fire?

Fire trucks had arrived, and the firefighters worked frantically to control the blaze and save people. As they extended a ladder toward the higher floors, Lewis tried to call to them, but fatigue overcame him. Using his last bit of energy, he shoved the container forward into the view of a fireman with a hose. They could check it for fingerprints, something to help them catch the arsonist.

Then, amid the chaos, Mom hastened through the crowd of people who had gathered. She cried as she hurried toward Christina and clutched her. Lewis closed his eyes, trying to listen to their voices. He wanted to hold onto his family a bit longer, at least until Mom noticed him.

Then he realized: no one else had reacted to the boy with the cat and the girl on the tracks. People had ignored them, oblivious. Only he'd noticed the two ghosts.

And everyone had ignored *him*, night after night, as he watched over Mom. He had remained unseen, except tonight by Christina.

*I am ghost number three.*

Mom held his sister. "How did you escape the fire?"

"Lewis helped me."

"But that can't be."

"He was here!" Christina said. "He saved me. He got me out of the window and..." Sobs blurred the rest of her words.

A firefighter rushing past Mom stopped long enough to shout, "Any more of your family in there?"

She shook her head. "No." The fireman moved on, not hearing the rest of her story. "My son died a few months ago," she whispered. "He was so sick. We couldn't save him." Mom held Christina close, gazing into the shadows. She seemed to sense his presence one last time. "Thank you, Lewis."

A peaceful calm radiated through him. His mission was complete. *It's time for my voyage.*

The End

# YVONNE VENTRESCA

Yvonne Ventresca is the author of the award-winning young adult novels *Pandemic* and *Black Flowers, White Lies*. In addition, Yvonne has written two nonfiction books and several stories selected for collections, including the previous IWSG anthology, *Hero Lost: Mysteries of Death and Life*. She is currently pursuing an MFA in Writing for Children and Young Adults at Vermont College of Fine Arts. You can learn more at YvonneVentresca.com, where she features resources for writers.

www.yvonneventresca.com
www.twitter.com/YvonneVentresca
www.instagram.com/yvonneventresca

# The Ghosts of Pompeii
## By Sherry Ellis

I wanted pizza, and I knew just where to find it. Italy! Mama said the people there make the best pizza ever. Except when I told my big sister, Squirt, that I wanted to go, she looked at me as if I had tomato sauce for brains.

"Bubba, what are you thinking? We can go to Papa Gino's and get some."

"But it tastes better in Italy," I said.

"How do you know? You've never been there."

"Mama says it tastes better. That's how I know. So there."

I made a face and stomped off to the woods behind our house. That's where the big hole was hidden, under the sycamore tree. I'd dug it with the magic shovel Grandpa Joe found at a garage sale. I knew it could take me to Italy because it had already taken me to China and Belize. It goes wherever I want it to go.

I stopped under the tree and stared at the pile of branches on top of the hole.

Squirt came up behind me. "You're seriously thinking about going through the portal for pizza?"

"I'm hungry!"

"What if something goes wrong?"

"What could possibly go wrong?"

Miss Worry Wart gave me her squinty-eye look. "Art thieves could lock us in a vault and leave us there to die. Or you could fall down a hole and land in somebody's grave."

I grinned. "Yeah. The grave in Belize was cool. But we're going to Italy. Not Paris. I don't think there are any art thieves there."

Squirt crossed her arms. "Well, you might get run over by a meatball."

I rolled my eyes. "Are you going to help me move these branches?" I asked as I picked up a few.

She huffed. "This is a bad idea."

"Whatever."

After the hole was uncovered, I grabbed a sled I'd propped against a tree. Sitting down on it, I pushed off and zoomed along the dirt chute as if it was a slide under the roots of the sycamore tree. It ended in a small dirt room.

Two seconds later, Squirt came down on her sled. "The only reason I'm doing this is because you can't go by yourself. You'd never make it back."

"Oh, yeah? That's what you think." I stuck my tongue out at her then stood in front of the wall in the back of the room. I shouted the magic word. "Al-eee-oosh!"

There was a blinding flash. A spiraling circle of blue and white light appeared in front of us—the vortex to Italy.

"Ready?" I asked.

"No!" Squirt said. "We forgot the..."

I didn't hear what else she said because I jumped right into the light.

The vortex whisked me off my feet into a tunnel with shimmering blue walls that rippled like waves. At the end was a bright light. I flew through the tunnel into the light. Then it became dark.

I landed with a thud. My hands stung as they scraped across the gritty floor. Dirt and dust tickled my nose. I looked around. Not much to see, because I was still underground, but up ahead was a dot of light—the way out.

"Squirt?" I called. "Where are you?"

I heard shuffling behind me. "Over here."

"Did you bring a flashlight?"

"No, Bubba. That's what I was trying to tell you. We forgot the flashlights."

I shrugged. It didn't matter. "The exit is up there. Let's get out of here and find the best pizza ever!"

Squirt made a grunting sound, but she followed me as I crawled forward over the rough ground.

Finally, we reached the opening. We got out and stood up.

"Whoa," Squirt said. "I don't think we're going to find pizza here!"

She was right. The place was a wreck—the remains of an ancient city. Crumbling stone buildings and pillars stood everywhere. Worn cobblestone roads crossed between them.

"Where are we?" I asked.

"No idea. Let's see if we can find somebody who can tell us." She looked around and pointed at a bronze statue of a man standing on top of a pedestal. "Remember that for when we come back."

We walked past the wreckage. Some buildings with pillars looked like they might've been fancy when they were new.

In the distance, a tall mountain rose up, as if it watched over everything.

Eventually we came to a grassy area. Rows of white pillars popped up, outlining what was once a huge building. A man with curly black hair and a mustache and beard stood next to one of the pillars.

"Hey look, Squirt. There's somebody."

I ran toward him, but then stopped.

"What's wrong?" Squirt asked.

"He's not a guy. He's a ghost!"

"What makes you think that?"

"Look at him," I said. "He's blurry. And check out his clothes. It looks like he's wearing a dress."

"A toga," Squirt corrected.

I looked at Mister Ghost. He didn't move. "Should we go up to him?"

Squirt shook her head. "Try waving and see what he does."

I raised my hand.

Mister Ghost raised his. He seemed friendly.

Squirt and I inched forward.

"Hi," I said when we were closer.

"*Ciao*," the ghost said back.

Chow? That sounded good. "Yes, please. We'd like some chow. Could you tell us where the pizza place is?"

Squirt gave me an elbow jab. "'*Ciao*' means 'hello' in Italian."

Mister Ghost smiled and walked toward us. "Hello," he said. "My name is Pliny."

Squirt scrunched her eyebrows. "Wait a minute. I know that name. Pliny the Elder?"

"*Sì*. Yes."

"The philosopher and commander of the army and navy in the Roman Empire a billion years ago?"

Pliny chuckled. "Not a billion years ago, but yes, the rest is correct."

I looked at Miss Smarty Pants. "How did you know that?"

"School. I learned about him in history class."

"Okay, Pliny. Could you please tell us where we are?"

"Pompeii."

"Pompeii?" Squirt's eyeballs almost popped out of her head. She pointed at the mountain. "Is that Vesuvius? The volcano that destroyed this place?"

"*Sì*. It was horrible."

"You were there?" I asked.

Pliny nodded. "August twenty-fourth. 79 AD. It started with an earthquake. Walls and roofs crumbled as we scrambled to get away. Then the volcano

23

erupted. Ash rained down. The sky turned black and the rotten stench of sulfur filled the air. We couldn't escape.

"I tried to save my friends by bringing them to my ship, but the winds wouldn't allow us to leave port. The ash became so heavy, I couldn't breathe. That's when I died."

I frowned. That sounded horrible. "I'm glad I wasn't there!"

"Unfortunately, Vesuvius is about to erupt again."

Squirt's eyes got big. "Seriously?"

"When?" I asked.

"Soon. Maybe today."

"Today?" Squirt put her hands on her hips and gave me one of her fire-breathing-dragon looks. "I told you this was a bad idea. You picked the worst day to come. We're going home, Mister Pizza-brains!"

"Good idea," Pliny said. "But could you let others know so they can evacuate? We wouldn't want history to repeat itself."

"Who are we going to tell?" Squirt asked. "And how are they going to believe us? We're just a couple of kids."

"You'll figure it out. I have faith in you."

And with that, Pliny vanished.

Squirt and I looked at each other.

"Does this mean we're not getting pizza?" I asked.

"Not unless you want it volcano-roasted. Come on. If we find somebody on our way to the hole, we'll tell them. If not, we're not going out of our way to do this. I'm sure they have some 'volcano about to blow' alarm. Let's get out of here."

On our way back, we saw an old man and a little boy walking toward us. They wore button down shirts tucked into baggy khaki pants. They weren't blurry, so I knew they weren't ghosts.

"Let's go tell them," I said.

"Wait. We need a plan. You can't go running up to people telling them the volcano is about to erupt."

"Why not?"

"Because they'll think you're crazy!"

I didn't care. I ran ahead. "*Cioa*," I said when I reached them. "How are you doing today?"

They stopped and looked at me as if I was crazy. The boy giggled. "You're dressed funny."

I looked down at my jeans and T-shirt. "No, I'm not. You are."

His brown eyes twinkled. "What's your name?"

"Bubba, and that's my big sister, Squirt." I pointed as she walked toward us. Her face looked as red as a tomato.

My name is Francesco, and this is my *nonno*, Giovanni."

"*Nonno*?" I asked.

"Grandpa."

Nonno smiled. The lines around his dark eyes crinkled. "*Cioa*," he said. "What are you doing here? Where are your parents?"

I told him the whole story.

Nonno frowned. "That doesn't make sense, young man. I think we need to take you to the police so they can help you find your parents."

"No!" I said. "We can show you where the hole is."

"I know it sounds crazy," Squirt said, "but Bubba is telling the truth."

Nonno shook his head. "I don't want to see the hole. Come with us. You can tell your story to the police."

I took a deep breath and let it out. Squirt glared at me. We needed a miracle to get out of this one.

Then something caught my attention.

"Hey, look!" I said. "More ghosts!"

"Where?" asked Francesco.

"Over there!" I pointed ahead. On the path in front

of us were two people—a lady and a boy. Dressed in togas, they were blurry. Just like Pliny.

That was good, because Nonno would believe us and not take us to the police station.

But he wasn't doing well. He looked worse than the ghosts. He got all pale and grabbed his chest. "Ghosts?" he whispered. "Where?"

"Right over there," Francesco said. "I see them."

I walked up to the lady ghost, who wore a long, white dress. Her long, curly black hair fell to her shoulders. I thought her the prettiest lady I'd ever seen. Except for Mama, of course.

"*Cioa*," I said. "I'm Bubba."

She smiled, her brown eyes warm and friendly. "*Cioa*. My name is Livia." She put a hand on the boy's shoulder. "This is my son, Drusus."

He was as big as me, with curly hair like mine but it was black instead of blond. He smiled.

"We have come to help you," Livia said.

"We heard the volcano might erupt," Squirt said, who had her arm around Nonno. "Is that what you wanted to tell us?"

"*Sì*. We want your friends to know, too. They have to help warn everyone."

Nonno crinkled his bushy eyebrows and made his eyes squinty. "I don't see any ghosts. Who are you talking to? What kind of game is this?"

Francesco pointed at the ghosts. "You can't see them?"

He shook his head. "I don't hear anyone, either."

Livia smiled. "Only children can see us. Your grandfather cannot. We need you to give the message to the adults. If you don't, you and many others will meet the same fate as us."

"What happened to you?" Francesco asked.

"Come. We will show you." Livia and Drusus turned and walked down the road ahead of us.

26

Francesco grabbed his grandpa's hand. "The ghosts say only kids can see them, but they are really there. They want to show us something. Come on."

We followed until we came to a roped-off area. Lying on the ground were the weirdest things I'd ever seen. Statues. Brown human statues. But they weren't standing up. They were lying there, all curled up or flat on their faces.

"Whoa," I said. "What are those things?"

"Those," Livia explained, "are the petrified remains of people who died when Vesuvius erupted and buried Pompeii."

I gulped. "Those were real people?"

"Sì. Two thousand people lost their lives that day."

"Are you a statue, too?"

Livia pointed to two statues on the ground ahead of us: A big person lying face-down on the ground and a small person curled up next to it. "Sorry," I mumbled.

Livia looked at me with kind eyes. "It's okay. We just have to warn everyone, so this doesn't happen again."

"Are the ghosts saying something?" Nonno asked.

"Yes," Francesco said. "The lady ghost pointed out her and her son's remains. She says we have to warn everyone that the volcano is going to erupt so we don't end up like her and the rest of these people."

Nonno frowned. "How are we going to do that?"

Squirt crossed her arms and shook her head. "No. The question is, why do *we* have to do that? This is the twenty-first century. Aren't there scientists who have machines that can tell when the volcano is going to erupt? Can't they warn everyone?"

"Twenty-first century?" Nonno raised his bushy brows. "I'm afraid you're mistaken, young lady. It's the twentieth century."

Squirt and I looked at each other.

"What do you mean?" Squirt asked. "What's the date?"

"March 17, 1944."

"Holy mackerel!" I shouted. "We went back in time?"

Francesco gave us a puzzled look. "What did you think the date was?"

"March 17, 2020."

Francesco and Nonno glanced at each other.

"Well," Francesco said, "I guess that's why you're dressed funny."

Livia smiled. "The eruption won't be expected. Now hurry. There isn't much time."

*Poof!* Livia and Drusus disappeared.

"The ghost told us the eruption will be unexpected," Francesco said.

Nonno frowned. "Then we'd better take her advice. We can go to the *Osservatorio* Vesuvio and notify the scientists there."

"The what?" I asked.

"The science station near the volcano that monitors its activity."

"Okay," Squirt said. "So, Francesco and you can warn the scientists and Bubba and I can get out of here and go home, right?"

I didn't like the sound of that one bit. "No! I want pizza!"

Francesco laughed. "Pizza?"

Squirt shook her head. "That's why we came. He wanted pizza in Italy."

Nonno smiled. "There's a restaurant nearby. You can come with us to talk to the scientists. Afterward, we can stop for a quick slice of pizza. Then we'll bring you back so you can go home. I want to make sure the story about the vortex you came through is true. Otherwise, you're going to the police and they can sort it out."

"Okay," I said. "Fair enough."

Squirt scowled, but she didn't object.

Nonno led us to a giant red car that looked as though it belonged in a museum. "A 1939 Alfa Romeo," he explained. "A beauty, isn't she?"

"Sure is," I said.

We piled in, and he drove us to the observatory. The old, reddish building with pillars looked like somebody's house. Not a science place. Inside, display cases containing old scientific tools and instruments sat in the middle of the brown tile floor. Along the walls in cabinets were rock samples. There was even a gold telescope on a wooden pedestal, which was set up pointing at one of the windows, but the window was covered with shutters.

"The observatory also serves as a museum," Nonno explained.

Francesco walked over to a display behind red ropes. "Check this out!"

It was a statue of a person lying on gravel. Another victim from Pompeii.

"Where are the scientists?" I asked.

"Maybe in there." Nonno pointed to a door in the back. It was closed, but the rustling we heard told us something was going on in the room behind it.

I went up to the door and banged on it. A tall man wearing glasses opened it and glared at me.

"Hi," I said. "Sorry to bother you, but we wanted to tell you the volcano is going to blow."

He didn't say anything. I peeked around him. Two other men stood in the room, huddled over a funny-looking machine.

"What are you doing?" I asked.

One of the men looked up and stroked his black, bushy beard. "Monitoring the seismic activity of Mount Vesuvius."

"The what?"

"The vibrations caused by earthquakes."

The man who answered the door finally spoke. "Why are you here?"

I told him again, because apparently, he had short-term memory loss. "The volcano is about to erupt. You have to get out of here and warn everyone."

The other guy scratched his hairless head and nodded. "We've had a lot of seismic activity, but it doesn't mean that the volcano is going to erupt. Would you like to see the activity our machine recorded?"

I nodded. Grouchy Man stepped aside, and we entered. I looked at the fancy machine. The pen on it drew spikey lines on the paper. "You guys can read this?"

"Sì. Look here." The bearded guy pointed to an extra-big spikey section on the paper. "This was an earthquake."

"See? We told you," Squirt said. "You have to get everyone out now! You can't wait."

Grouchy Man made another frowny face. "Evacuation is a big ordeal. Everyone within a fifteen-kilometer radius would need to leave. Thousands of people. You have to be sure before you send that many people on the road."

Francesco's eyes widened. "Where will we go?"

"To a different part of the country. Far away from here. It'll take a week to move everyone."

Squirt crossed her arms. "Then you'd better get started, because you won't have that long before it erupts!"

"What makes you so sure?" Grouchy Man asked.

"We have our sources."

Grouchy Man opened his mouth to say something else, but he was stopped by a loud, grinding sound. It came from the fancy machine. It shook and stopped moving.

The bearded man next to it frowned and said

something in Italian.

Nonno wrinkled his eyebrows. "What happened?"

The hairless guy glanced up. "The seismograph broke."

That was bad news, because they wouldn't be able to tell what was going on with the volcano until it was too late.

We had to think of something to convince these guys to evacuate.

We didn't have to think long, because what happened next was amazing. The brown statue lying on the floor drifted through the door and hovered right in front of us.

Everybody's mouths dropped open.

"Look, another ghost!" Francesco shouted.

He was right. A blurry man wearing a toga stood behind the floating statue.

"I know you grown-ups can't see him like we can," Squirt said, "but you can see what the ghost is doing. He's the one making the statue hover. Other ghosts told us to warn you about the volcano. That's why we are here. Please believe us."

Grouchy Man looked whiter than the ghost. So did Nonno.

Mister Bearded Man took a deep breath. "I believe you. We'll sound the alarm and begin the evacuation."

I clapped my hands. "Yay!"

The statue body drifted back out to its original place and landed gently on the ground. The ghost waved, and then he vanished as quickly as he'd come.

"Now can we get pizza?" I asked.

Nonno's color returned to his face. "Maybe a slice to go. But we need to hurry. Who knows how long we have?"

We said goodbye to the scientists who got right to work sending out the evacuation order.

On the way back to Pompeii we had a problem,

though. The ground shook, and the car jiggled from side to side. Earthquake!

Nonno's eyes grew big. "Sorry, kids. No pizza! We're taking you right back. We all need to get out of here."

We got to Pompeii and hopped out of the car. The place was deserted. We walked past the crumbling old buildings. Squirt led the way. I hoped she knew where she was going.

Suddenly, we heard a loud bang. We whipped around and gasped. A giant cloud of smoke blasted out of the top of Vesuvius.

"It's erupting!" Squirt shouted.

"Yes, it is," a voice behind us said.

I turned around. Pliny!

He looked at Francesco. "You must leave now. I will lead Bubba and Squirt back to the hole. Hurry!"

Francesco told Nonno what Pliny had said.

"Sì," Nonno said, not needing to be told twice. "Arrivederci, children!"

I ran up to him and gave him a hug. "Arrivederci, Nonno!"

Nonno squeezed me back. Then he took Francesco's hand and ran.

"Are they going to be okay?" Squirt asked.

Pliny nodded. "Sì. But you two need to hurry." He stretched out his arm, showing the way before disappearing.

We ran along the cobblestone road. The ground shook under our feet.

"Look!" Squirt shouted, pointing. Ahead of us were two white, glowing figures—Livia and Drusus! They waved their hands, telling us to follow.

"Over here," Drusus called.

Livia stood near the statue on a pedestal we'd seen when we first arrived. She pointed to an opening in the ground near her feet. "There it is."

We scrambled in. "Thank you," we shouted.

When we got to the end of the tunnel, I yelled the magic word. "Al-eee-oosh!"

The ground shook. A spiraling circle of blue and white light appeared on the wall.

"JUMMP!" we said and plunged into it, headfirst.

We flew through the tunnel. At the end sat a bright light. We passed through it and fell to the ground.

I opened my eyes and let them get used to the dark. "Squirt," I called. "Are you okay?"

I heard a groan behind me. "Bubba, we are never doing another one of your crazy ideas again. Got it?"

Even though I couldn't see her, I knew she was making a growly-bear-face at me. I wasn't going to argue.

"Let's get out of here," she said.

We grabbed our sleds, climbed up past tree roots to the opening, and crawled out. No volcano or crumbling old buildings. Just the familiar woods behind our house.

Squirt picked up some branches. "Let's cover this thing. And cover it good, because I don't ever want to go down there, again!"

"What? But it was fun!"

"Fun? You call earthquakes and an erupting volcano fun?" Squirt's face was as red as a tomato. I tried not to laugh, because she looked like a pizza.

"Well, the volcano and earthquake weren't fun, but the ghosts were!"

Squirt rolled her eyes and threw big branches over the hole. I grabbed a couple, too. Soon, the whole thing was covered.

"Okay," Squirt said. "Let's go home."

When we got inside, Mama was washing dishes. She stopped when she saw us. "Where have you two been?"

I shrugged. "Outside saving the world from a

big, bad volcano." I looked down at my clothes and brushed off some dirt. "We'll go clean up. When we're done, can you make us pizza? Like the one you had in Italy?"

Mama scrunched her eyebrows. "Margherita pizza? Sure." She took another look at us and shook her head.

Squirt and I changed and made ourselves clean and shiny. When we were finished, the pizza was ready.

"It has the colors of the Italian flag: red tomatoes, green basil, and white cheese," Mama said.

"It's good," Squirt said after taking a bite.

"Did you know the first pizzeria was created by a chef in Naples, not too far from the volcano, Mount Vesuvius?" Mama asked.

I stopped chewing and looked up. "Mount Vesuvius?" I couldn't believe it. We were just there!

"In 1830, he lined his oven with rocks from the volcano and baked a pizza."

A real volcano-roasted pizza.

"Mama?" I asked. "When was the last time Mount Vesuvius erupted?"

"March 18, 1944."

Squirt and I looked at each other. The day after we were there.

"Do you know if anybody died?" Squirt asked.

"Let me look it up." Mama pulled out her smartphone. "It destroyed three villages, and the United States Army 340th Bombardment Group lost about eighty aircraft. But it says only twenty-six people were killed. Twelve thousand were displaced. The warning must've come out in time to save the rest, so it wasn't as horrific as what happened in 79 AD."

I didn't like that anybody had died at all, but I was happy that what we did helped save many lives.

I looked at Squirt. She smiled.

I didn't want to stop going through the hole. I'd go again. And maybe—just maybe—Squirt would come, too.

The End

Award-winning author Sherry Ellis is a professional musician who plays and teaches violin, viola, and piano. When she's not writing or engaged in musical activities, she can be found taking care of household chores, hiking, or exploring the world. She lives in Atlanta, Georgia.
www.sherryellis.org
www.bubbaandsquirt.org
www.facebook.com/Sherry-Ellis-388897186076
www.twitter.com/513sherrye

# The Blind Ship
## By Bish Denham

**"I** am loathe to have you leave, but your father insists you go to him."

"I'll be fine, Mother." Jacques was impatient to board *Le Rôdeur,* the ship that would carry him to his father on the island of Guadeloupe in the Caribbean. His father owned a sugar cane plantation there and the boy was eager not only to be with his father, but to learn about the running of the profitable business. He wanted to follow in his father's footsteps.

His mother turned from him and spoke to Captain Boucher, a burly man well into middle-age. "You will look after my son?"

Before the gentleman could answer, Jacques said, "I am not a child, Mother." Though only twelve years-old he had, since his father's going to Guadeloupe, considered himself the head of the household.

Captain Boucher laughed and placed his large hand on Jacques' the boy's shoulder. "Be assured, Madam Romaigne, young Jacques will be well taken care of. And, if he is interested, I will teach him the ropes of sailing the ship."

Jacques saw that his mother's eyes glistened as she nodded slightly. "My husband, in his letters to me, assured me you are an honorable man and your ship seaworthy."

"Indeed, Madam. Your husband and I are well acquainted. If something should happen to Jacques, I would be held responsible and so I take him into my charge knowing he is the most precious cargo I will have on board."

Jacques worked hard to keep from fidgeting,

uncomfortable with being discussed by the adults as if a mere child of six. Despite the chill of January, the docks at Le Havre, a port in the Normandy region of northwest France, were noisy with men loading or unloading cargo from the numerous tall-masted, wooden sailing ships. All the activity heightened his senses and Jacques wanted to run about and explore like a puppy. The air smelled of sea, animals, sweat, and human refuse. Though he thought of this journey as a grand adventure, he knew his mother feared for his safety.

His mother turned back to her son, "Mind your manners," she said as she brushed imagined dust from the shoulder of his jacket. "And obey Captain Boucher.

"Of course, Mother."

"I have something for you." She handed him a book. It was a journal, bound in fine Moroquin leather of a deep gray with gilded fleur de lis at each corner of the front cover. "I want you to write in it every day and describe your journey. If I follow you next spring, I would like to read it."

"Thank you, Mother." Jacques turned the journal over in his hands. It was a perfect gift. "If you follow?"

"You know I am afraid of the ocean, Jacques. And, there are other issues that make me uncomfortable about leaving France."

"But Father misses you!"

"As I miss him and as I will miss you. But..."

"It is time," Captain Boucher interrupted. "The tide turns and we must be away."

Jacques saw it was all his mother could do to keep from weeping out right and so he didn't mind that she embraced him tightly and kissed him on the cheek.

* * *

The journey from France and along the western coast of Africa was uneventful. Despite a calm sea and favorable winds, Jacques was seasick the first few days and teased by some of the crew, even Captain Boucher. But most particularly by Cook, who placed savory meals in front of him which only caused Jacques to excuse himself from the table.

Jacques wrote in his journal, *The ship's surgeon, Monsieur Gagne, has assured me I will feel better soon, but at the moment I could throw myself overboard.*

He had difficulty sleeping as he was not used to the noises the ship made: the creaks, squeaks, and moans of the wood, the slap of sails against the masts, the slosh of waves against the hull, the calling and talking of sailors on deck.

But by the third day he felt well enough to venture out of his cabin. The fresh, windy air quickly revived him and he soon gained his sea legs.

*M. Gagne was right! I am now quite well and am looking forward to the rest of my journey. You must not worry about me, Mother.*

\* \* \*

*On March 14th, we anchored at Bonny, a port on the Niger Delta in the Bight of Biafra. Captain Boucher expects to be here at least three weeks.*

*Bonny is an island nation ruled by a Negro king. It is a busy port. Tomorrow Captain Boucher is taking me to the home of Monsieur Dumont where I will be staying while Captain Boucher conducts his business.*

M. Dumont was a wealthy man and Jacques relished sleeping in a real bed with clean sheets and eating off plates that didn't slide around on the table. M. Dumont's son Hugo, a young man of 18, entertained him and took him about town and showed him many interesting sites, including one of the slave markets.

*I did not care for the slave market, Mother. I cannot help but feel the Negros are human beings and not cattle. They weep and cry and suffer just as terribly as any of us. I saw a mother have her child, a boy no*

38

*older than myself, pulled from her arms. She and the boy were both quite distraught. I have tried to imagine how I would feel in that situation and it is quite beyond me. After seeing that I asked Hugo to take me back to his house. I did not sleep well last night because of vague dreams of being carried away against my will.*

\* \* \*

*At last we are on our way,* he wrote a few days later. *Le Rôdeur is 200 tons and we now have on board 160 Negro slaves.*

Jacques reread his words. He had already commented on the fair weather carrying him toward the Caribbean. He tried not to think about what lay in the close dank, dark quarters of the hold. It was enough that he could hear their muffled moans and cries through the decking.

He took up his quill and continued writing.

*I know you will miss me while you tarry in France, but father needs me on the plantation. Besides, I long to see the green hills of Guadeloupe and the blue waters of the bays. Take heart, Mother, soon you will follow and we will be together once again.*

At dinner a few days later, M. Gagne and Captain Boucher spoke of shipboard issues. Jacques, as a paying passenger, ate with the men. They talked over his head, as if he wasn't there.

"The slaves have brought ophthalmia on board with them," said M. Gagne.

"Ophthalmia?" asked Jacques. "What is that?"

"An eye disease that causes blindness." said M. Gagne. "At worst the blindness is permanent. Most often, if treated properly, vision will return, though in some cases one's sight will be impaired."

"How bad?" asked Captain Boucher.

"It is spreading at a frightful rate. There are already more than I can manage."

"I cannot afford to lose my cargo, Gagne. Every

slave cured is worth his value."

"I would request," said the surgeon, "that I bring them on deck where I can more easily attend them."

Captain Boucher agreed. "But only twenty at a time, for fifteen minutes."

The next morning the human cargo was brought up from the hold.

Even though he was not an officer, Jacques was allowed on the quarterdeck provided he kept out of the way. From there he could look over the stern and watch the mesmerizing wake or gaze towards the bow across the upper deck and marvel at the agility of the sailors or see the naked misery crawling out of the dark depths. The women and children were brought up first.

They were at first confused and disoriented, huddling together and squinting in the brightness of the sunlight. But soon they basked in the sun as sailors threw buckets of seawater over them and M. Gagne examined them.

When the third group came on deck, Jacques noticed a woman with a young child in her arms. It was obvious the child was either dead or unconscious as its limbs hung loosely from its body. The mother, in a state of hysteria, wept and wailed in a way that made him shiver even as the sun beat down on his head.

The mother wrenched herself free from a sailor who tried to pull the child from her arms and ran to railing of the ship. She paused, looked back over her shoulder at the other women, then threw herself, child clutched in her arms, over the side. Her dark form disappeared beneath the foam. It happened so quickly the sailors couldn't stop her.

Jacques heard a scream.

"Get the boy below!" Captain Boucher bellowed. Before he could be half dragged, half carried below deck, three more slaves followed the first into the sea. Only when tossed on his bunk did Jacques realize the screams came from him.

Several days passed before Jacques ate or came out on deck. His dreams were nightmares that revisited what he had witnessed. He debated writing about it in his journal, but in the end found comfort in imagining his beautiful mother listening to his pain.

*They would rather plunge to their deaths than be in chains,* Jacques wrote. *I try to imagine if it were you and me in that position and cannot even bear to think of it. Captain Boucher has ordered that all the slaves remain in the hold.*

The next day he wrote: *The disease is spreading at a terrifying rate. M. Gagne declared the cases are already so numerous as to be beyond his management. The sailors sling down provisions to the wretches from the upper deck as they are afraid of coming in contact with the disease.*

Dinners with Captain Boucher and M. Gagne became tense, silent affairs. Jacques took to eating in the galley where Cook told him wild stories of pirates and buried treasure, shipwrecks and haunted islands. But none of his stories eased the sickening misery in the hold which multiplied a thousand times when M. Gagne announced all the slaves had the disease.

*Mother, both Captain Boucher and M. Gagne are complaining of blurred vision and some of the crew have already lost their sight. I dread going to sleep at night and dread waking in the morning because I know the day will only bring more suffering. And what if the disease begins to affect me?*

The waves rolled on carrying the ship on their endless heaving backs. The sunlight and wind no longer refreshed or felt clean to Jacques. He no longer enjoyed looking out over the stern of the ship to be mesmerized by the wake. All he could think of were the people who littered the waves.

*I rose this morning,* Jacques wrote, *to find Captain Boucher, M. Gagne, and the first mate completely blind! So far, I have been spared. But will it always be so?*

And, a few days later, *All the crew, save one, a sailor named Louis, is blind. Captain Boucher preserves what order he can, and M. Gagne still attempts to do his duty, but we are in a frightful situation. The crew works under Louis' orders. They move about like unconscious machines. Captain Boucher stands by with a thick rope, which he sometimes applies to the back of a pitiful sailor if Louis tells him the man is unfaithful in his duty.*

Jacques took it upon himself to serve Captain Boucher and M. Gagne. As Cook was also blind, he fixed what meals he could, or helped the two men to the quarterdeck. With him and Louis the only ones still able to see, he used his eyes to the best of his ability. He guided sailors from chore to chore and lent a hand where he could, washing the deck or coiling rope.

In the hold the slaves groaned and cried.

* * *

Jacques woke one morning terrified, for he found his own vision blurry. *In a little while I shall see nothing but death,* he wrote. *I will write as long as I can, Mother, but I, too, could go blind.*

*Something must be done for the misery in the hold.*

The stench from the conditions below deck wafted up through the decking, permeating the air and sticking to everything from wood to clothes. Jacques wondered if there would ever come a day when the odor left his nose.

His eyes failing, Jacques felt his way to the upper deck and went to Captain Boucher, who stood with rope in hand. Louis stood by his side and bawled out orders to the blind crew that shuffled listlessly about.

"Captain," said Jacques, "Can nothing be done for the Negroes in the hold?"

He turned his sightless eyes towards the boy. "What would you have me do when we can scarcely care for ourselves?"

"Could not some of them be allowed to come up on deck? Perhaps the fresh air would ease some of their agony."

"My crew is as blind as those creatures. Should we bring them up they might well throw themselves off the ship as they did before, and we would not be able to stop them. Is that what you want? Better to leave them where they are. At least a portion of them will be saleable, *if* we have the good fortune of reaching Guadeloupe."

"But sir..."

"Away from me, boy! I must try to save my ship and crew."

Jacques and the crew despaired of ever seeing the light of day again.

Each lived in his own dark world of misery. Jacques felt his way about and managed to find biscuits, dry and hard as stone, which he softened in a cup of water. He considered himself fortunate knowing unfed cargo suffered below.

One morning, Louis, the only one with eyes to see, gave a dire warning. "I sense a storm brewing."

He yelled at the men to prepare as best they could. They stumbled and groped blindly for ropes and hatches.

By evening the storm came down upon them. Captain Boucher ordered everyone below. Only Louis remained at the helm to somehow pilot the blind ship as it got tossed on the heaving waves.

Jacques clung to his bunk to keep from being thrown to the deck.

"This is how it ends," he thought. "The ship will

sink and I will be drowned at sea. I am sorry, Mother."

They flew like a ghost ship, the masts cracking, sails snapping and bursting from their bonds. The noise was like the sharp report of muskets. One moment they were swallowed in the troughs of the angry sea, the decks awash with livid spray. The next it cast them up to the crests as if vomiting the ship out of its bowels.

Jacques prayed fervently for it to end, that their lives be spared.

Hours and hours later, dawn broke over a dull, dark gray sea, and the wind began to die. The ship wallowed, floundering and directionless. Louis reported most of its sails were in tatters and a forward mast broken. He had not slept or rested in more than 24 hours.

Late in the afternoon, Louis yelled out words Jacques thought he'd ever hear. "A sail, I see a sail!"

He steered the ship towards it as best he could.

Jacques, like many of the crew, stumbled blindly to the side, his heart bursting with hope they would be saved. He heard noises upon the sea, the sound of water sloshing against a wooden hull that was not their hull. A cry went out from every mouth on deck, echoed by those lying in their hammocks below.

And from deep within the hold, the human cargo cried for rescue.

Their cries were answered, voices carried on the wind as if on the wings of birds.

Captain Boucher was the first to recover his speech.

"Ahoy! Ship ahoy! What ship are you?"

"The *Saint Leon* from Spain," a voice called back. "Help us, for God's sake. We are dying of hunger and thirst. Give us provisions, name your terms."

"We need help ourselves!" Captain Boucher cried in disbelief. "We will give you provisions if you will give us some of your men."

"Money! We will pay you money, a hundred times over for food and water. But men we cannot give for we are all stone blind and would be useless to you!"

A horrid silence fell between the ships. It was as if death had thrown his shroud over them, muffling all sound.

But then, one the crew on *Le Rôdeur* began to laugh. It spread like the blinding disease itself and soon the ship was in a state of awful merriment. Laughter gave a morbid kind of release, for the coincidence was more than they could bare.

Jacques, too, laughed. He found himself down on the deck, doubled over, clutching his belly. He could not stop himself.

The Spaniards cursed them as the blind ships drifted apart.

* * *

*Mother, your son was blind for ten days! But now I am able to see well enough to write. We have lived in a world peopled by shadows. We could not see the ship or the heavens or the sea or the faces of our comrades. It has been a horror, yet somehow we are only a day or so away from Guadeloupe.*

*While on the quarterdeck this morning I overheard a conversation between the first mate and Captain Boucher. They did not take notice of my being there.*

*'Are you quite certain the cargo is insured?'*

*Captain Boucher said, 'I am. Every slave that is lost must be made good by the underwriters. They have cost us enough already. Do your duty.'*

The next day Jacques was horrified to learn what that duty meant. In the dead of night, Captain Boucher had ordered 39 blind slaves tied with weights and thrown into the sea.

*Perhaps, if I had known, I could have said or done something to stop it,* he wrote. *I dread having to look*

*Captain Boucher in the face, but I intend to ask him why.*

"Because," Captain Boucher replied without emotion, "they were unsalable and it was senseless to keep them."

"If they had all become blind would you have thrown all of them into the sea?" Jacques asked.

"These issues are none of your concern nor will I have a mere boy question my decisions and authority."

* * *

*It is due to Louis alone that we are now only a few leagues from Guadeloupe. What a brave and gallant soul he is. Captain Boucher has lost an eye. M. Gagne and eleven of our 22 crew are blind for life and five are able to see but dimly. Among the slaves were those 39 who were drowned for being sightless. The rest are either blind in one eye or their vision is impaired.*

*As for me, I seem to be recovering.*

*I have heard you talk, Mother, when you did not think I was listening, with some of the ladies who visit you. I have heard you speak against slavery. I did not think anything of it at the time. I thought it was silly woman's talk. I thought you did not understand how Father makes his money and that if we did not have slaves to work the plantation on Guadeloupe, we would not be able to live as we do.*

*"But now I think I understand why you have been so hesitant to come to the island. It is not because you do not love my father, I know you do as I know he loves you. It is because of slavery. You do not want to witness it. You do not want to seem to condone it when your heart tells you it is wrong.*

*You are right in your beliefs. Slavery is an evil that must be abolished.*

*I know I am just a boy in the eyes of many, but I have seen things no man should see.*

*Mother, as God as my witness, I will try to convince*

*Father to sell the plantation and return to France. If he refuses, know that I will return to you as soon as I can. Perhaps together we can find a way to put an end to this madness called slavery.*

\* \* \*

Jacques stood at the bow of the ship and watched the green hills of Guadeloupe rise from the sea. As the battered ship made its way into the harbor of Pointe-a-Pitre, he was grateful to God to be able to pick out his father where he stood on the dock. He was anxious to set foot upon solid ground and smell the clean sweet air.

Yet even as he stood, wildly waving, a dark shadow hung over him, for he dreaded the confrontation to come. And under his feet, deep in the hold, he heard the slaves' muffled moans. He knew their journey and ordeal was not over, would never be over, and that his life would never be the same.

Author's Note: Though I have taken great liberties, this story is based on actual events as experienced and written down in the journal of twelve year old Jacques B. Romaigne between January and June of 1819. In June the following year Benjamin Constant, a French politician and author, gave an impassioned speech against slavery to the French Chamber of Deputies, quoting from Jacques' dictated account of what he witnessed on board *Le Rôdeur*, including the slaves being thrown overboard. The poet, John Greenleaf Whittier, was also inspired by Jacques' account, and wrote the anti-slavery poem "The Slave-Ships." Opthalmia was a general term used to describe a variety of highly contagious eye diseases which caused inflammation of the eyes that could lead to blindness or impaired vision. As for the Spanish ship, the *Saint Leon*, she was never heard from again.

The End


Bish Denham is from the U.S. Virgin Islands, where her family has lived for over a hundred years. The author of two middle grade novels and a collection of retold Jamaican Anansi stories, she says, "Growing up in the islands was like living inside a history book."
www.bish-randomthoughts.blogspot.com
www.facebook.com/BishDenham.Author
www.goodreads.com/author/show/6439315.Bish_Denham
www.twitter.com/BishDenham

# Dare, Double Dare
## By Louise MacBeath Barbour

"**I** dare you!"

Sara barely considered her brother Kelsey's challenge. "I double dare you!" she shot back.

Their father's car had just turned out of the driveway onto the paved road.

"This is our chance. Unless you're scared."

"Not!" Sara stared down her brother from across the round maple table. But he crossed his eyes, and she broke eye contact, laughing. "Not fair. You always win like that."

"If you focused you might win. Shall we do this—finally?"

Sara looked out her great-grandmother's front windows at the pouring rain and dark clouds. The only colorful things visible in the soft light were the antique blue, green, and brown bottles standing on sills below the windows. Outside, wind lashed the trees, and rain drummed on the windows, running down the glass in rivulets.

Their parents and great-grandmother had just left for Halifax and wouldn't be back until the evening. Now that she was eleven and Kelsey twelve, their parents felt comfortable leaving them alone for the day—with stern warnings to behave, of course. Besides, plenty of relatives lived nearby in the Cove.

"We haven't anything better to do," she said.

"Then let's go!"

He pounded up the steep stairs to the landing and wide hallway. Sara ran up after him before she lost her nerve. Kelsey pushed aside a table and lamp, and they both dragged out a trunk blocking a door.

"Better take that flashlight," Sara said.

Kelsey grabbed it from beside the lamp and stuck it behind his waistband.

Sara had no idea what to expect behind the forbidden door. If you didn't know it was there, you might miss it. The door and hinges were painted the same white as the rest of the hallway, the forged-iron handle usually hidden by the trunk.

"I'm glad there's no lock," Kelsey said. He pushed the thumb latch down and pulled on the handle. "Dude, this is stuck. It must be warped."

"I wonder how long it's been since anyone opened it," Sara said, watching him tug on the handle.

"A while, I bet. This house is over two hundred years old." Kelsey braced his foot against the baseboard, gave the handle a yank, and the door flew open. "Boy, is it dark in there!"

"We're in big trouble if we get caught."

"No one's going to catch us. Mom, Dad, and Great-Grammie are gone all day. You're not chickening out, are you?"

"You're not exactly rushing in."

Kelsey pulled out the flashlight, turned it on, and swept its light around the dark space. They spotted a bare bulb hanging from the ceiling just inside the door. He tugged its pull-chain up and down several times.

"No such luck," he said with disgust. He stepped into the dark room and beckoned for Sara to follow.

They walked around the room examining the walls and floors. Kelsey probed the corners with the light. Dust and dead flies littered the plank floor.

"There's nothing here," Kelsey said.

"What about that weird thing around the chimney?"

"I think it's a smoker closet. Great-Grammie said they used to smoke hams up here when she was little."

"Let's check it out."

They stepped inside the small enclosure, and Kelsey ran the light over the ceiling. "Look at those big hooks. That must be where they hung the hams."

"There has to be something here. Why else would Great-Grammie forbid everyone from going in this room?" Sara began pounding on the walls.

"What are you doing?"

"Listening for hollow spots. You check the floor." The two banged and stomped around the smoker closet.

"I think I've got something, Sara! There's a small handle bolted to the floor. See? Close to the wall. I bet it's a trapdoor." He got down on his hands and knees and ran his right hand over the floor. "It must have hidden hinges."

"No way!" Sara said. She knelt beside him in a nook between the chimney and the wall. "Can you open it?"

Kelsey pulled up on the handle, and the trapdoor yielded slightly. "Not another warped door," he groaned. "Can you get your fingers under the edge?"

Sara squeezed her fingers into the crack and tugged while Kelsey pulled on the handle. Together they forced the trapdoor open. He shone the light down the hole, illuminating a ladder that descended below the stone foundation of the house.

"You're not going down there," Sara said.

"Yup. Shine the light for me."

Kelsey handed the flashlight to Sara and swung his legs into the narrow space. He placed his feet on the second rung of the ladder and braced himself with his arms in the trapdoor opening, slowly putting his weight on the third rung.

"So far, so good," he said.

Kelsey caught the top rung with one hand and

stepped down farther. Then he scrambled down.

"Drop the flashlight and climb down. I'll light your way."

Sara followed and landed on a dirt floor. She stood in a pitch-dark space, except for the narrow cone of light emitted by the flashlight.

"Now what?" she said.

"We look. Like you said, there must be something here." He turned around in the empty space.

"It's about ten foot square," Kelsey said as he moved the light around.

"Give me the flashlight for once. Just because you're older doesn't mean you get to hold it all the time."

"I let you hold it up there."

"Give. Me. The. Light!" Sara stepped toward Kelsey and felt something under her right foot. "Give it here. There's something in the floor."

Moving her foot, she shone the light on a small disk half-buried in the dirt. She tucked the flashlight under her left arm and squatted. She pried the disk out, spit on it, and rubbed it on her jeans to remove the dirt. Then she held it in the light.

"It looks like an old coin!" she exclaimed. "I think it's silver. I can make out '1600' and three fleurs-de-lis. This must be an old French coin."

"1600? That's way older than this house."

"I wonder how it got here. Maybe Dad can tell us more about it." Sara pushed the coin into the front pocket of her jeans and swept the light along the lower walls.

"There!" Kelsey said.

He knelt and inspected a grate across an opening in the wall opposite the ladder while Sara bathed it with light. He yanked the grate out of the way and peered into the opening.

"Give it here," he said.

Sara grimaced and handed over the flashlight.

He shone the light into the opening. "There's a tunnel and some light up ahead, maybe forty feet."

Sara crowded close to look. "It's like a secret passage."

"Someone went to a lot of work to brace it with wood." Kelsey took a deep breath. "There must be an opening where that light is, because the air seems okay. I'm going to see if I can reach it." He crawled through the hole and into the tunnel.

"If you think I'm going to stay here by myself, you are so wrong."

"Watch out for creepy-crawlies."

"Oh, yuck!" She crawled after him toward the faint light. "Where do you think this comes out?"

"Maybe by Uncle Charlie's workshop."

They continued on their hands and knees through the narrow passage. Kelsey barged ahead with the light and Sara followed, batting the odd root out of her face.

"Here's another grate," he said. "And this one is locked on the inside."

"Great! I don't want to back up all the way to the ladder. I just want out of this creepy place!"

"No worries," Kelsey said. "There's a key." He lifted it from a hook screwed into a timber above the grate and turned it in the lock. "And, it works!"

He pushed the grate out and wriggled through the opening.

"Have you got the key?" Sara called after him.

"In my pocket."

Sara crawled out, replaced the grate, and stood up. She brushed the dirt off her clothes and looked around. A brook gurgled past the small hillside they had emerged from. "Where are we?"

"Nowhere near Uncle Charlie's workshop," Kelsey said.

"The rain stopped," Sara said. "It's not even wet and look at the trees. They're really big and really old. There are no trees like these around Great-Grammie's."

"Or around Nova Scotia that I know of," Kelsey added.

"I think I see water beyond the trees over there. Let's go that way."

A few minutes later, after pushing through some underbrush toward the glint of water, they walked into a clearing that sloped to the shore a few hundred feet away. A wide basin of water opened up to their right, and a river flowed into the basin on their left. An island stood not far offshore in front of them. The water glittered in the bright sunlight, and green wooded hills lined the blue basin.

"I know it's not possible," Sara said in an awed whisper, "but this looks like the Annapolis Basin from the North Mountain side."

"That's miles from Great-Grammie's house. On the opposite side of the basin. Where are the fields and houses? All I see are trees."

"I swear that's Goat Island," Sara said. "So that's got to be the Annapolis River. Which means Annapolis Royal is that way." She pointed upriver toward the northeast.

"Let's walk down to the shore and see if we can get our bearings," Kelsey suggested.

They crossed the clearing, dodging stumps and deep piles of branches. When they reached the water's edge, they looked up and down the shoreline.

"See!" Sara said. "I'm right! That's Bear Island down there." She pointed southwest down the basin.

"If that's Bear Island, where are the people?"

Sara scanned the basin and the hills. Unbroken forest covered the land. Nothing was on the water.

"Something is very wrong," she said, looking at

Kelsey as fear unfurled inside her and her hands began to sweat. "There is no sign of people anywhere."

"No kidding. But it's getting late in the afternoon, and we need to figure something out quickly."

"Afternoon? Mom, Dad, and Great-Grammie just left a while ago. In the morning."

"Look at the sun. It's not morning anymore." Kelsey sank down on a large rock like someone had sucker-punched him in the stomach.

"It's useless to stay here," Sara said. "Let's walk toward Annapolis. There must be houses around that point. We can call home from one of them."

She started walking along the rocky beach toward a bend in the shore where the trees came down to the water. Kelsey caught up with her. The sun beat down on them, and Sara longed for a drink of water.

As they neared the trees, an older girl burst out of the woods running toward them, waving her arms and shouting gibberish. She came to an abrupt stop when she got close, then started backing away from them. Her dark eyes darted between Sara and Kelsey. They stared at her speechless.

Sara recovered first. She took in the girl's brown skin and flowing dark hair, her loose tunic and long skirt made of soft skins, her moccasins, and the shell necklace around her neck.

"Mi'kmaq?" she asked tentatively.

"E'e," the girl answered. She was breathing hard from running. "Jacques," she said more forcefully and pointed to the woods. She gestured for them to follow and ran back into the trees.

They plunged into the forest after her. The sudden gloom after the dazzling sunlight was disorienting, and Sara hoped she wouldn't trip and go sprawling before her eyes adjusted. The Mi'kmaw girl ran deeper into the woods, angling back in the direction they had come from.

Kelsey passed Sara and gained on the girl. "Keep up," he yelled. "We can't lose her."

"I am," Sara yelled back, running faster.

Without warning, Kelsey and the girl stopped. Sara almost slammed into her brother.

Directly in front of them was a large black bear, and behind her, two cubs. One of the cubs reared up on its hind legs and looked at them while the other froze on four paws. The mother bear shuffled her feet and moved her great head back and forth. Her black nose at the tip of her brown snout sniffed the air repeatedly.

Kelsey lifted his arms high and wide and stepped forward.

The girl turned toward him and raised her right palm. "Arrêtez!"

"Don't move," whispered Sara, her gaze glued on the bear.

The mother bear lunged forward and suddenly stomped, slamming her feet on the ground and blowing air out explosively. Everyone stopped breathing.

The bear drew her upper lip down making her muzzle look longer and laid her ears back. She charged at them blowing loudly. Then she stopped abruptly and clacked her jaws several times before backing off a few steps.

"I think she's bluffing," Kelsey said. He stomped the ground, raised his arms, and roared at the bear.

The cubs darted up a nearby tree, and their mother chased after them. She turned at the base of the tree, stood her ground, and clacked her jaws several times again.

"You idiot!" Sara hissed. "Don't you know a mother bear is dangerous when you threaten her cubs?"

The bear charged and retreated several times. The strange blowing noise she made as she rushed at them grated on Sara's ears, and the jaw clacking was downright freaky.

The Mi'kmaw girl began speaking firmly to the bear. Never once looking the bear in the eyes, she backed away sideways. The bear remained on the ground by the tree with her cubs and watched them.

Sara mimicked the girl, sidling in the same direction. "Back off, Kelsey," she said quietly.

The three of them backed away slowly. When they had retreated a ways, the Mi'kmaw girl said, "Jacques," turned, and started walking in haste. When the bears disappeared behind enough trees, she broke into a run. Kelsey and Sara chased her again.

"There's a guy lying by a tree," Kelsey shouted as the Mi'kmaw girl dropped beside a still form.

"He's unconscious," he said when he reached them. "Jacques?" he asked the girl.

"E'e."

"He's not Mi'kmaq," Kelsey said. "He's a little older than the girl."

"His arm is bleeding," Sara said as she knelt opposite the girl. "What happened?"

"Il est tombé." Fighting tears, she pointed up at the tree and let her hand fall to the ground.

Sara looked up. "He fell? Out of the tree?"

The girl reached up, tapped the tree, and dropped her hand again. Then she jumped up and dashed off.

"Oh, great!" said Sara. "She dumped him on us and took off."

"Forget about her. This guy needs our help."

"Okay. Um—"

"Is he breathing?" Kelsey asked as he crouched by Sara.

"I'm not sure. See if you can feel his breath." Sara relaxed a little, remembering what their parents had taught them.

Kelsey placed his cheek close to the lad's mouth. After several seconds he said, "Yup."

"Pulse?"

"Yup."

"Anything broken?"

Looking down and up Jacques' body, Kelsey said, "I don't think so."

"Try shaking him."

"Hey!" Kelsey gently shook Jacques' shoulders. "Are you all right?" He smacked Jacques' cheeks lightly. "Wake up!"

Sara cradled Jacques' arm and eased his bloody sleeve up to check his wound. Dark red blood welled up along a gaping, jagged gash. "Give me a strip of your T-shirt. Quick!"

As Kelsey slashed around the bottom of his T-shirt with a Swiss knife, the girl returned wringing handfuls of sphagnum moss. She pressed it against the gash. Sara bound his wound with the strip and lifted the bandaged arm above the level of Jacques' heart.

"Go, Doc!" Kelsey teased, grinning at her.

"Don't look at me like that!" Sara said to Kelsey. "I read it in a book, okay?"

After an anxious few minutes, Jacques stirred, and Kelsey said, "I think that's working." He signaled to the girl to help him prop Jacques against the tree trunk while Sara kept his arm above his heart.

"Aimée?" Jacques gasped. She answered rapidly with words that neither Sara nor Kelsey understood.

"Easy, Dude," Kelsey said to him. Jacques looked from him to Sara and pushed back against the tree. He spoke to Aimée, gasping for breath between short bursts of words.

"I think I heard 'Habitation,'" Kelsey whispered.

"They must be historical interpreters from Port-Royal, dressed like the era of the Habitation. That explains his woolen breeches, those knit stockings, that baggy shirt."

"Then why is he lying here in the woods with no help?"

"Are you from the Habitation?" Sara said.

"Anglais? Vous-êtes anglais?" Jacques said.

"Yes. Oui."

"Vous parlez français?"

Sara shook her head. "Très peu."

"Je parle...un peu d'anglais. A little English."

"Is the Habitation far?" Kelsey said. "Can we get you out to a road? Flag down a car?"

"Help me," Jacques said. "Aidez-moi au bord de la forêt."

He struggled to rise, and Aimée and Kelsey helped him to his feet.

"Edge of the forest? Dude, we'll get you to the Habitation."

"Non! You aren't from here. They won't understand."

He turned to Aimée and spoke a mishmash of words. She nodded and took off running.

"When I tell you to hide: cacher," Jacques said. "Cachez-vous! Promettez-moi ça!"

"We promise," Sara said, slipping under his injured arm and supporting his shoulder. "Let's get him moving, Kelsey."

The three hobbled along, pausing frequently to let Jacques catch his breath. Woody debris covered the ground. Pits, formed where trees had fallen over exposing their roots, and mounds of decaying trunks blocked their way. But Jacques knew where to go.

Sara watched as the sun descended and worried about the approaching twilight. At last they stumbled onto a path of sorts.

"Let me stop here," Jacques said. "Aimée... arriver...soon. Avec others."

They helped him sit on a log that had fallen against a large rock.

"Écoutez attentivement! Listen. Over there." He pointed to a huge boulder dropped by a melting glacier. "Big rock. Shelter. You hide there. Cachez-vous! Do not let them see you!"

"He's serious, Kelsey."

"If no one comes soon, we're coming back," Kelsey said to Jacques. "Are you sure you'll be okay?"

"Oui." Jacques closed his eyes and leaned against the rock. "Allez."

They raced for the huge boulder.

"Oh, wow," Sara said when they scrambled around it. "Someone's built a lean-to."

They looked at the heap of spruce boughs draped over a branch supported by two Y-topped stakes. The boughs overlapped the branch onto a ledge in the glacial erratic.

"Don't get comfortable," Kelsey said. "We're going to follow them and figure out what's going on."

"Shhh! Someone's coming."

They peered into the shadowy distance from around the boulder. Aimée led four men along the faint path to where Jacques rested: two Mi'kmaq men wearing leather breechcloths and leggings and two men dressed like Jacques. They lifted him up by his shoulders and knees and hurried back along the path.

"Come on," Kelsey said. They followed the group as quickly and as silently as possible.

About twenty minutes later they reached the edge of the forest. The Habitation stood in a clearing studded with stumps. Well-tended vegetable gardens grew between the fort and the shore. The air carried the smell of woodsmoke and roasting meat across the clearing. All at once, they were ravenous.

Sara and Kelsey watched the men carry Jacques around a palisade of tree trunks stuck in the ground. They scurried after them, running low along the bottom of the palisade. Peeking around a corner, they saw the men lugging Jacques through an open gate.

They snuck through the gate and slipped behind several large casks by some stairs leading to an upper level—just in time to see Aimée enter a building of rough-sawn boards across a dirt courtyard. A commotion broke out as the men carried Jacques in.

"We need a better spot to hide," Kelsey whispered.

"Quick! Up these stairs!"

Sara ran up to the landing, flattened herself against a wall of bark-covered upright logs, and glanced around an open door. She motioned for Kelsey to come and disappeared inside.

Seconds later Kelsey reached her, and they looked around a dim room. Stacks of casks, baskets, and furs stood on the floor, a birchbark canoe rested on a table, and furs and skins hung on the walls.

"Where's the flashlight?" Sara said.

Kelsey patted himself down. "I must have dropped it."

"Oh, great!" Sara hissed.

"This looks like a storeroom."

"No one's here. If we're careful, we might be able to see what's happening."

Sara tiptoed to one side of the door and Kelsey to the other. They ventured a peek outside. The building Aimée and the others had entered sat adjacent to the storeroom building.

Kelsey belly-crawled to the rails of the landing and looked toward the lamplit room Jacques was in.

"I can't see anything but legs of people and legs of furniture," he whispered. "I'm hearing French and possibly Mi'kmaq."

Sara slid beside him, surveying the courtyard and the other buildings. Lower and smaller than the building next to them, their walls were constructed with upright tree trunks. Bark and some roughly-hewn planks formed the roofs.

They backed up into the storeroom and leaned against the upright logs of the wall. Kelsey closed his eyes briefly, rubbed his face, and looked at Sara.

"We're so screwed," he said.

"This is no reconstruction, and those people aren't interpreters imitating Habitation life for tourists," Sara replied.

"No, they aren't. This is like 1605 or 1606."

"Now what?"

"Let's get away from this door. Hide better. Think." He pointed to furs piled behind the casks and baskets. "Over there."

Just as they were about to flop onto the soft furs, someone grabbed them around their necks and clamped hefty hands over their mouths. As they flailed and kicked, they were forced to the floor. The calloused hands and strong arms pinned their heads to the thick planks.

Sara looked sideways at Kelsey, at his wild eyes. She thrashed harder, but the relentless arm and hand held her down.

Kelsey stopped moving, stared at Sara, and widened his eyes. She ceased struggling. After several moments their assailant removed his hands, and they sat up and faced the man squatting on the floor.

Like the other Mi'kmaq, he wore a breechcloth, leggings, and moccasins. A few feathers adorned his headband. But that's as far as the similarity went. He was a big, strong man with long arms and legs; and unlike the Mi'kmaq men, he sported a dark beard like the Frenchmen. His piercing eyes gazed at them from a stern, grave face.

"Shhh!" he said, laying an index finger against his lips.

"Membertou," Kelsey gasped.

"Membertou? The Mi'kmaw chief who befriended

the French at the Habitation?" Sara said.

"Silence!" Membertou ordered.

He jumped up and hauled Kelsey to his feet. Pinning him with one arm, he searched Kelsey's pockets with his opposite hand and found the heavy brass key.

Sara lunged at Membertou and caught his free arm. She gripped an end of the key with one hand and tried to jerk it out of Membertou's fist.

"You and your darn dare," she yelled at Kelsey. "I should never have listened to you. I wish I were back in Great-Grammie's front room right now. I—"

Sara's stomach lurched, and nausea washed over her. Dizzy and disoriented, she hung on to Membertou's arm and the key. She watched in shock as something fell in slow motion and shattered on a floor. Her great-grandmother rose from the table by her windows lined with the familiar bottles. Membertou still grasped Kelsey to his side, and Sara still clutched his other arm and the key in his fist. They abruptly let go of one another, and the key fell to the floor.

Moving faster than Sara thought possible, their great-grandmother rushed into her bedroom off the front room and returned holding an old Mi'kmaw pipe. She approached Membertou, pressed the pipe into his hands, and wrapped his fingers around its stone bowl and long wooden stem.

Then she stepped back and commanded in clear, deliberate French, "Pensez à l'habitation!" She tapped her forehead and repeated, "Pensez!"

Membertou nodded, smiled slightly, and vanished.

Astounded, Sara gaped at the spot where the chief had stood. Only the key and the shattered teacup remained. She looked around at her great-grandmother's front room. They were home.

Their great-grandmother pointed at the table and

said, "Sit. We need to talk."

"Where are Mom and Dad?" Sara asked, hesitating.

"Home. They were dead tired after driving up to Halifax in bad weather and chauffeuring me around to appointments. They left a little while ago, figuring you must have gone home to raid the refrigerator."

"We should—"

"Don't interrupt me, Sara." She pointed to a chair, and this time Sara sat down. "I've only had time to go up and see if the window screens were closed to keep the mosquitoes out. As soon as I saw the trunk, I realized what might have happened and came back down. Why couldn't you obey me and not go into that room?"

The phone rang shrilly, and their great-grandmother picked up the receiver. She listened briefly and said, "Don't worry. They're here. They had quite a day." Great-Grammie glared at Sara and Kelsey. She listened to the voice at the other end and added, "Let them spend the night, Maggie. They're really tired." She paused a moment, then continued, "I'll heat up some leftover beans for supper. It's no problem, dear."

Kelsey laid his head on his arms at the table and closed his eyes.

Sara rested her chin in her hands and her elbows on the table. "Beans sound so good," she said.

Their great-grandmother hung up the phone, swept up the teacup, and sopped up the tea. She retrieved the key and hung it on a hook in the kitchen. Then she rummaged in the fridge for supper fixings and put the beans on the stove to heat. She filled the kettle and plugged it in. Fetching three teacups and a tea cozy, she placed them on a tray with milk, ground ginger, and a teapot.

Sara listened to the soothing sounds of her great-grandmother in the kitchen. When she placed the tray on the table, Sara said, "May I help, Grammie?"

"Be a good girl and get some silverware and glasses of water."

Sara set the table, kicking Kelsey's foot when she plunked his silverware on a placemat in front of him. "You could help, you know. Just because Great-Grammie treats boys like princes and girls like servants doesn't mean—"

"She thinks boys are extra special," Kelsey said, kicking her back.

"She thinks you're stupid," Sara jeered into his upturned ear. "She thinks boys and men should be catered to. Then she runs her household and them."

"You're just jealous. I get leftover pie. You get leftover bread." He sat up, folded his arms against his chest, and grinned.

"Are you two at it again?" their great-grandmother asked as she put down two bowls of beans. The delicious smell of molasses and bacon rose with the steam.

"No," they said.

"I hope not." She lifted the teapot, snug in its tea cozy, and poured two cups of tea. She stirred in some ginger and a generous amount of milk and handed them the teacups.

"Not ginger tea," Kelsey groaned.

"Drink it. It's good for what ails you."

"Nothing ails me!"

"You and your sister have just traveled four hundred years back and forth in time. That would unsettle anyone. Drink, eat, and then we'll talk."

"How—"

"Eat."

They devoured their food, helping themselves to extra beans and homemade bread. Three big slices of raspberry pie also disappeared and more of the dreaded ginger tea.

"Now, tell me what happened. Don't skip anything."

When Sara described finding the old coin, her great-grandmother interrupted, "Do you still have it?"

Sara took it out of her pocket and placed it on the glossy tabletop in front of her great-grandmother.

Night had fallen and their great grandmother switched on the lamp centered on the table in front of the windows. She picked up the coin and turned it over in her fingers. Her blue eyes sparkled in the lamplight, and for a moment, Sara could see the young woman she had once been.

"This is what took you back there," she said. "In the right hands, an object like this can be a powerful talisman."

"What do you mean?" Kelsey said.

"Show me your foot."

Kelsey balked. Then he shrugged and removed his sneaker and sock, setting his bare foot on the floor in front of her.

"You see your two toes on the outside of your foot? How they curve inward against your other toes instead of being straight?"

"So? Sara has the same toes."

"So?" his great-grandmother snapped. "Listen, young man. Having toes like that is a trait that passes from generation to generation in our family. Sometimes it skips one. Sometimes it doesn't. You're the only ones in your generation who have curved outer toes."

"Mom has them," Sara said.

"Yes, she does. She's the only other one of my descendants who has this trait."

"Why is that important?" Kelsey asked, more politely this time.

"Those of us who have this trait also have the ability to move through time—"

"That's crazy!" Kelsey interrupted.

"Were you not just here with Membertou? At the real Habitation?"

"How could you know that?"

"Because I have the same toes, and I've been there too."

Kelsey sank back in his chair.

Sara stared at her great-grandmother, that proper fire-and-brimstone Baptist lady who never missed a sermon on Sunday morning, calmly discussing time travel.

"My husband, Kelsey, your great-grandfather, was the real traveler in the family. He could travel at will. The few times I went back, I had to concentrate on an object like this coin. Or," she added, "I could hold on tight to Kelsey and travel with him."

"You could travel in time, and you only went back a few times?" Sara said.

"It's dangerous. You never know what you'll step into. I quite like my own place and time. It's where I belong. But Kelsey," she paused as tears flooded her eyes, "Kelsey was a traveler. I think you two are also. You managed to go and return without knowing what you were doing."

"Oh no," Sara said, jumping up and running into the parlor. She knelt by a black fur rug that had lain on the floor forever. She picked up its large head with a brown snout and glass eyes.

"It was you in the woods. With your cubs." She forced back tears and returned to the front room. "This is a dream. I'm dreaming I saw that bear in the woods."

"Your great-grandfather returned with that bearskin one time. He would never tell me how he came to have it."

"Do you think we can go back?" Sara asked her great-grandmother.

She nodded.

"Can we find out what happened to Jacques and Aimée?" Kelsey butted in.

"You don't have to go back in time to find that out. They're your many times great-grandparents."

"And the tunnel under the house that comes out on North Mountain?" Sara said, remembering the eerie passage.

"It doesn't always come out there, and once you get better at moving in time, you won't need it."

Kelsey looked at the old French coin with an expression of awe and respect on his face. Then he met Sara's eyes and said, "I think we have some interesting times ahead of us."

The End


Born in Nova Scotia and raised throughout eastern Canada, Louise is a writer and blogger who lives with her supportive husband in Colorado. She writes fiction and nonfiction. Her love of reading, photography, geology, and travel rounds out her enthusiastic embrace of life."
www.selkiegrey4.blogspot.com
www.facebook.com/mlouisebarbour

# Return to Cahokia
## By L.T. Ward

"**T**onalli, my daughter," my mother calls, "have you prepared yourself for our journey?"

"Yes, Mama," I tell her. Mama knows my siblings and I are all ready for our return to Cahokia. It has been nearly eight months since our last visit, and we are—literally—bursting with anticipation to return.

Since our departure from our summer home, my family has traveled long distances over the earth to reach the dark, chilly waters in the east. We rode the clouds south toward the warmer climates—our duty as the Warm Weather gods. We spent our winter lounging and resting over the lands, providing the luxurious humidity and heat our people need. As we winter over the southern lands, they reward us with offerings of their bountiful harvest. Cocoa is my favorite, but my mother, Yolotl, loves the offering of guava.

But now, spring approaches, and we get to finally return to our favorite home.

"Come along, Tonalli," my mother says. I follow her obediently, walking with care atop the clouds. My father, Yaxkin, never joins us. He has to remain behind to lighten the days, reflecting his warmth to his brother, Meztli, to brighten the nights. Mama will guide us, though. My many siblings and I make the journey every spring to Cahokia without Papa, but he visits as best he can. He usually makes time several weeks in the late summer, just before we prepare our eastward trek to the sea. And he will join us for the Arrival Celebration.

Mama moves over the clouds with grace, barely

looking at her feet as she steps from one to the next. Tekakwitha, however, catches her toes on a white tuft, tumbling into a roll of thunder. Rightfully so, my sister was named for her inability to avoid collisions. Without my brother Wayra's winds sent ahead, warning of storms, Tekakwitha's clumsiness startles our people below, sending them rushing to their shelters, hiding from the harsh weather that doesn't come.

Helping Tekakwitha rise from her foot trap, I say, "Come on, sister. A few more days, and then we will be at Cahokia!"

Smiling, Tekakwitha says, "Do you think they will offer rhubarb again this year?"

Shaking my head, I tell her, "Probably not. Our Cold Weather cousins did not head north during early spring as they usually do. I fear the springtide fruits have been spoiled by their antics." The Cold Weather gods typically remain at Cahokia throughout the autumn and winter, but this year, they refused to leave on time to their northern home. They stayed too long, their frosts and snows slowing the return of blossoms to the trees.

Pouting, Tekakwitha stares at her feet, leaping with care onto the next cloud. She lands quietly as a light breeze.

"I'm looking forward to playing Chunkey," Inti says. My brother looks so much like Papa, but where my father shines, Inti is all about play. Only under Mama's supervision does Inti do what he is supposed to. It is his games that break through our storming clouds. Our people love him for his streams of light, giving them inspiration during our familial storms. If only they knew it was Inti's misbehaviors that gave them their beloved streak of light.

My brother Ehecatl smiles mischievously. Tauntingly, he says, "Inti, are you looking forward to me beating you again?" Inti has never beaten Ehecatl in Chunkey. But Ehecatl is a cheater. When the spears are thrown at the rolling stone, he blows his winds to either knock his opponents' spears away from the target or his own closer to it. Technically, Ehecatl isn't breaking the rules of the game, but I don't think it is fair for him to use his winds to win.

After a long day of travel, the white clouds have filled with the dust from our feet and the sweat from our brows. "We will need to rest," Mama says. She bends toward her feet, gently dragging her slender hand into the gray cloud at her feet. My siblings and I move toward the ripples she creates. The light grays of the cloud change to darkness. Tekakwitha traces the edge of Mama's circle with her fingers. A rumble beneath our feet commences. Wayra and Ehecatl pucker their lips, blowing the dirt loose from the cloud.

On the earth below, our people race to their shelters. Our sweat begins to trickle free from the cloud, warning of the storm we are bringing. Tekakwitha kneels, pressing her palms against the floor of our cloud, wringing free more of the rains.

Inti and I take our positions beside Mama and the darkened tufts. With a tap of my finger, a bolt of light flashes toward the earth. Tekakwitha slaps the cloud, shaking loose her thunder as well as more of our sweat. Inti, on Tekakwitha's other side, taps twice, followed by my sister's slaps. More lightning. More thunder.

My siblings and I work to clean our cloud from the stress of our day's journey. Mama watches over us. When our cloud is finally emptied of our sweat and debris, Mama lightly touches our shoulders, telling us to stop. The cloud has returned to its thin white fluff. She pulls back the whitened tuft, making small burrows for my siblings and me. Mama tucks

71

us into our comfortable bed, allowing us to sleep until the next morning's sunrise, when we will resume our hike to Cahokia.

* * *

The next few days, we travel, ridding our clouds of debris every few hours. We do not sleep until Tío Meztli has risen, our storms continuing into the middle of the night. Reactions from the people below are mixed. Some are relieved to see our sweat falling, nourishing their seedling crops. Some are upset, fearful of my brothers' winds or Inti's and my lightning.

But our clouds are expected. All our people say prayers, thanking us for the end of winter, thanking us for bringing forth the promise of summer.

By our third day of travel, we all grow tired. Cahokia is another day and a half away, and we are ready to be there.

"Oye!" shouts a voice behind us. My family pauses in our steps, turning to see my cousin Tupac leaping like a vicuña from the clouds behind us. "Wait for me!" he says, waving his arms overhead.

My favorite cousin reaches us, slowing his gait to our pace. Tupac is our fastest family member. He is one of the Warrior gods and Papa's most trusted messenger.

"Tía Yolotl, Tío Yaxkin sent me ahead. Khuno is coming. He is to join you at Cahokia this summer," Tupac says.

"If that is what Yaxkin wants," Mama says. "When should we expect my nephew?"

Tupac tells us, "Early tomorrow morning, Tía Yolotl."

"And will you be joining us as well?"

Shaking his head, Tupac says, "Tío Yaxkin wants me to return home. It is a busy summer ahead and I am needed there."

"Thank you for your message, Tupac. Tell my

72

husband that we will prepare for Khuno's arrival," Mama says. She hugs Tupac farewell before he turns toward the sky in the southwest. "My children, we must prepare for your cousin's arrival."

"But Mama, our people will be angry with us," whines Tekakwitha.

Petting my sister's cheek, Mama says, "I know, my daughter, but your father knows best. If Khuno is to join us, we must welcome him." Looking to the rest of us, Mama says, "My children, we will slow our pace. We will rest until Khuno arrives."

Pouting, Tekakwitha flops herself onto the cloud. Thunder growls from beneath her. My brothers and I do the same, more cautiously than my frustrated sister.

Purging our cloud of the day's grime will also have to wait. There will be no more storms until my cousin's arrival.

* * *

Through the evening and into the night, our cloud drifts along, swelling from our collected dirt. There is no more sleep. The cloud is too filthy. It has filled and become too lumpy for peaceful slumber. Instead, it floats, dropping the occasional rumble from Tekakwitha shifting in her seat, or rolls from one of my Wind brothers' frustrated sighs.

But by late morning, Khuno arrives from behind us.

"Oye, Tía Yolotl!" he calls. "Oye, cousins!" Khuno's steps are heavier than Tupac's. He treads from one cloud to the next, but where Tupac's clouds remained floating in their original paths, Khuno's rush forward in short bursts from his cumbersome footing.

Once he is one cloud behind us, Mama greets my cousin, "Oye, Khuno! We have been awaiting your arrival." She smiles gently at Khuno, holding a tender place for him in her heart. One of the original goddesses, Mama was named for her exceptional ability to love. Even Khuno, whose presence means hardships on those around him, Mama could not help but love.

Turning back to my siblings and me, Mama says, "My children, it is time." Mama kneels, rippling the massive black cloud with a swish of her hands. My Wind brothers bend to the cloud. Pressing their cheeks to the fluff, they blow. Hard. Tekakwitha digs her hands into the cloud, burying her fists up to her wrists. Inti and I plow our ten fingers into the cloud, charges of lightning bouncing throughout the cloud.

Then Khuno leaps onto our cloud.

With the landing, his feet sink into the blackened tuft, and he loses himself until he wears the cloud as a skirt. Khuno kicks his feet within the fluff, spinning himself gracefully. His whirlwind spins him around. When Khuno is spiraling so fast that his face blurs before our eyes, he reaches for the edge of the cloud. Khuno grips the rim hard, pulling himself out of the whirlwind. Our cloud funnels toward the earth below.

Our people scream.

They scatter to find their loved ones. To herd their livestock.

They run for their shelters.

As Khuno's tornado drops to the earth below, Mama kneels, staring through the eye of the storm toward our people. Watching the tail of the tornado scorch the earth, Mama weeps. Her tears fall to the earth, hardened icy tears.

More screams from our people.

Mama's tears dry up. She raises herself from her knees, standing over us, nodding. We know it is time. Khuno stands beside Mama, watching his funnels bounce from the ground, dissipating until only our sweat drips from the clouds.

Inti and I retract our fingers from the cloud while

Tekakwitha does the same. Wayra and Ehecatl lift their cheeks from the tufted surface, both working hard to slow their breath. My siblings and I are exhausted, and our sweat trickles toward the earth.

"You did well, children," praises Mama. Under Papa's beaming light, our formerly noir cloud shines brightly. Mama says, "Time for rest." She glides over the cloud, tucking us in for a nap. We are allowed to sleep until the next tornadic storm.

When afternoon ends, Mama wakes us and Khuno. We must leave our cloud to make the distance to Cahokia. Mama leads the way as my siblings and I follow. Khuno stays one cloud behind until after Papa has finished his colorful goodnight to our people, filling the sky with ominous tangerines and eerie shadows of our family's journey.

As Tío Meztli rises for his nighttime watch, Mama tells us, "It is time for Khuno to join us." We ready ourselves across our filth-ridden cloud. Khuno leaps to the center, spiraling his funnel to reach toward the ground. Under the darkness, our people have little warning. Mama's tears fall, weeping for our lost people. But it is what must be, and we mourn along with Mama, our own tears dropping to the earth along with our sweat.

This second tornado finally ends, and we look back over our shoulders, watching our people search for their loved ones, searching for their scattered livestock and belongings. They pray to us that we bring forth no more storms. Some curse in our names. Some plead for our help. All pray that Tío Meztli gives the sky back to Papa, wanting the protections of the Great Sun.

"No more storms, children," Mama says. "Not until we reach Cahokia." We nod, sitting quietly as we watch our beloved people.

\* \* \*

Papa returns to the sky. It is our last day of travel. It is the day my family is eager for each year.

As our cloud drifted, Mama has remained vigilant, watching the skies beneath. Flocks of birds begin to accumulate. Ducks and cranes congregate. Mama smiles. She puckers her lips, placing a kiss into her palm. She blows her affections toward the flocks. The swarms of birds simultaneously nosedive toward the earth. Just before crashing into the ground, the birds somersault. They tuck their heads protectively beneath their wings. As they roll to their feet, they rise. Human.

The males are adorned in leather sandals and buckskin tunics and leggings. Their long black hair is single-braided away from their faces. The females dress similarly, although they wear longer dresses instead of tunics and their own obsidian hair splits into two braids. Mama's bird people continue their migration toward Cahokia. Our caravan has begun.

Once Mama has collected several hundred commoners, she searches the skies for additional servants. She selects from the roaming kites, hawks, and eagles several dozen to become our attendants for the summer. For our most essential and honored bodyguards and priests, Mama finds peregrine falcons. These are Papa's favorite birds and the ones he inspired the artisans to carve into the tablets, bowls, and jewelry to be presented at Cahokia. Each falcon receives one of Mama's kisses. Each honoree wears a leather strap around his neck, a sandstone charm with the carved Birdman dangling over his breast.

Our caravan traverses the earth. Mama pinches the edges of the cloud. She balls the tuft between her hands then drops it toward our bird people below. During the descent, the fluff hardens, transforming into the supplies we will need when we, ourselves, take human form. Our tents, our foods, our clothing. All of our items come from the cloud.

"Are you ready, children?" Mama asks, her smile reaching her eyes. We eagerly nod. "Tonalli and Inti, it is time." The others encircle my brother and me. Our cloud has dwarfed from Mama's efforts. Inti and I kneel across from one another. We gently align our fingertips to the other's. Sparks bounce between our hands.

"Wayra, you may go first," Mama says. My brother steps toward Inti and me. He climbs over our extended arms until he is standing between us. Inti and I press our palms together. A bolt of lightning cracks and Wayra disappears. From the hole in the cloud, we can see him waving back up. Wayra laughs heartily. He loves riding the lightning to the earth.

Then it is Tekakwitha's turn. My sister lands as she does everything else, in a crash. Khuno fares better than Tekakwitha, only stumbling a step upon landing. Ehecatl, though, is graceful. His feet hit the ground and he walks tall, assuming his regal position in the caravan immediately.

"Inti and Tonalli, you are ready," Mama says. She cups our paired hands. The sparks transfer to her palms. Inti and I release our grip on one another. I rise from my knees, stepping closer to Mama. She places the sparking crown near my head, and I am speared toward the earth. My heart races with excitement. I feel my humanity return, my body gaining the weight I do not feel when I am in the sky. I feel the dirt beneath my leather sandals when my feet land. I know Cahokia is close and the anticipation swells inside me until I giggle.

Ehecatl shoots me a warning look. It is not appropriate for such childish reactions from the second eldest in my family. However, I shrug him off, looking ahead as I walk to the front of our line.

Inti is moments behind me. His stride falls in beside mine. As the Sun children, we must walk together.

Mama lands ahead of us. The sky above contains no more clouds. Papa shines brightly on his Heart. Mama is elegant. Her raven hair is pinned into a knot at the nape of her neck. Copper orbs dangle from the lobes of her ears. Her dress is fitted, embroidered in fine woolen threads. Several falcons in flight are sewn across her skirt while the Great Sun is featured across her belly. Seashells, noting our family's wealth, are intricately stitched into the storytelling of her garb. From her shoulders, a long cape streams to her ankles. The white leather accents Mama's beautiful tan skin. Bright rainbow-inspired beads, made from the stones collected from the lands and seas of our travels, fringe the cape's hems.

Most impressive is Mama's headdress. Fine beads of reds, teals, and golds decorate the headband fastened over Mama's brow. Vibrant blue and green plumes protrude in a semicircle from the headband, extending wider than her shoulders. Her regal crown weighs heavily, but Mama strides effortlessly before us. Her head is high as the queen approaches the perimeter of Cahokia.

The roar of thousands of our people carries on the air as we approach. They have spent weeks trekking over the lands to arrive at our summer home. Over the next hill, our people will come into view. We will come into their view.

A stray shadow lays before us, a blackened streak extending from the sky to the earth. Mama leads our massive caravan toward the darkness. Her foot touches the dark ground, disappearing into the absent light. The sun is momentarily eclipsed into blackness. Mama emerges from the shadow and the cloudless sky returns. A towering man appears at

Mama's side.

Papa.

My father reaches for my mother's hand. He kisses it lovingly, dropping it to take his place at the front of the line.

Papa does not wear a cape as Mama does. He wears a similar headdress, the plumage tipped in the golds of his light. His kilt is equally as ornate as Mama's, weighted with intricate designs of the sun. Yellows, reds, and oranges brighten the leather. Papa's hair is pinned similarly as Mama's, and his earlobes encircle copper earrings. His skin shines from the oil coating his powerful muscles. The sun tattoos on his shoulders glisten under his light from above, appearing to dance as the muscles shift from his movements.

My heart swells with pride and anticipation while watching my parents.

My family crests the hill. Hundreds of tents have been erected. Thousands of people move about their temporary shelters. Our people have been waiting for us.

As we pass through the community, our people pause in whatever tasks have busied them. From the corner of my eye, I see their eyes widen and their mouths hang open. Mothers hush their children from excited squeals to see my family returning to Cahokia. We leave a wake of reverent silence.

The Great Mound cuts the horizon. Over the warm greens of the lands, we approach the layered pyramid. We pass several smaller pyramids. These belong to the tribal chieftains and priests of our people. My family and our caravan pass these important people. They kneel, as only the elderly and the highest ranking may remain standing. Those still on their feet bow their heads.

Papa reaches the meadow containing our pyramid.

Our bird-people commoners and servants fall back in our procession. They stand, watching as only my family, our bird priests, and our peregrine bodyguards continue forth. Our people's tribal chieftains and priests fall in line at their backs.

His foot on the first step, Papa begins his ascent of the pyramid. He climbs the stairs to the first landing. Mama is three steps behind, her cape hiding her steps from view. Inti and I ascend with our siblings and cousin immediately behind. The first landing is midway up the pyramid. I step to the right, turning around to face our congregation. Inti does the same to the left. My sister joins me. My brothers and cousin join Inti.

We watch the rest of our holy men and leaders pass by. They will join Papa and Mama at the top of the pyramid. Our peregrine bodyguards remain at the base, forming a wall of exceptional warriors. Each of the four sides of our pyramid is lined with a dozen stoic servants.

From my perch on the landing, I watch the eyes of our people. With my goddess eyes in my human body, I stare at our reflections in their eyes, enjoying the sight of my parents ascending their pyramid. I see Papa reach the top of the Great Mound. He takes several strides on the landing, turning to watch the rest of his procession join him. As the others assume their positions behind the Great Sun, Papa stands with his arms crossed over his broad chest. His face shows no emotion. I try to do the same.

The last priest finds his place behind Papa, at the northern edge of the pyramid top. Facing the south, the Great Sun raises his arms toward the light he has left above. He turns his head upward. From the depths of his belly, my father calls toward the sky. Three *harrumphs*.

From behind the Great Sun, his holy men and

leaders echo his calls. From his side, his wife does the same. From midway down the Great Pyramid, his children and nephew repeat the calls.

Papa lowers his face from the sky above to look toward our people.

I stop watching our reflections in their eyes. I watch their faces. They feel the same pride and excitement I do. From their mouths, three *harrumph*s echo my father's. The roar is deafening.

The Great Sun has ushered in this year's Arrival Celebration. By the next morning, Papa will return to his place in the sky, but here, summer has returned to Cahokia. From atop the mounds, my family will rule. There will be ceremonies, religious and celebratory. Our family will provide the weather necessary to encourage the crops to thrive. Our people will thank us with their bounty and their respect.

Life will be good for all, now that the Warm Weather gods have returned to Cahokia.

The End


LT hails from the Land of Corn, otherwise known as Central Illinois, where weather inspires her literary works. When not writing speculative fiction shorts and novels, she spends her days raising a brood of plague monsters (a.k.a. her children) as well as satisfying her never-ending thirst for knowledge through reading, meeting people, and first-hand life experiences.
www.twitter.com/Ltward2

# Feathered Fire
## By Roland Clarke

**T**he sun sun warmed the world as Vasy's goats nibbled the coarse grass. Light sparkled on the winding Berezina River. A tree stump in the sandy forest clearing gave Vasy the perfect place to tend her friends and watch.

On the far bank, the Nazis were unloading explosives and weapons from trucks. Guns they would use to kill her Soviet comrades. These invading vipers must be driven from her Motherland.

Their noise drowned out forest life. They had felled trees and levelled a track to the water's edge. They were assembling a bridge from boats and pre-built parts.

"They forget us partisans," she said to the goats, to the land, and to the sky. "We can stop them."

She gazed at some birds flying high above her. Was her older sister, Kalyna safe? Her heart swelled, proud of her pilot sibling who brought terror to the enemy. The Germans feared her and her female comrades, calling them *Nachthexen*—Night Witches. They rode the night winds to bomb fascist lines.

Maybe targets like this encampment.

But Kalyna was many miles away. When this war ended, they'd be together again. For now, Vasy would dream and forget her own fear of flying.

Work first.

Vasy finished counting the troops, the gun positions, and the armoured vehicles cluttering the far bank. She'd learnt to count the chickens on their farm, nine years earlier. Her throat tightened, but she stifled her memories.

Just remember the numbers. Anyway, writing anything down was dangerous.

The surprise Nazi build-up had to be important. Her comrades needed to know.

She walked into the pine trees, re-tracing her zigzag route back to the hidden partisan camp.

A bird attracted her attention as it looped over the herd.

"It's *Zharptica*," she told Zoya, the mother-goat. "I wonder if we should follow."

She knew the nanny wouldn't answer, but her imagination kept her dreams alive. The bird wasn't the mythical Firebird either. Vasy's father had taught her what hoopoes were—with their long, thin bills for probing the ground for insects. She must push the memories of her parents away, though. Well, their execution as 'counter-revolutionaries'. Why had she survived?

Better not answered. Dreams were her escape.

"When the Firebird suns herself with her wings open, she might leave a feather. A magic feather that takes us on an adventure."

Zoya just stared up at her. An accusation and a warning. The clever animal companions in the fairy tales warned the hero not to take feathers. Stealing was wrong—when to survive.

But she would be the heroine Princess Vasilisa. At twelve years old, Vasy was wiser than any boy or hero. She'd take a feather and avoid the enemy traps and tricks—with Zoya's help.

The bird had settled on the dusty ground of a clearing to spread its wings and bask in the afternoon sun.

Vasy leant against a tree and waited. Watching a mythical creature was more fun than watching fascists.

In a letter, Kalyna wrote she had painted the

Firebird on her plane. As children, they learned the *Zharptica* folklore from their mother.

Tears returned with the memories of losing Mama and Papa. They had hidden her and Kalyna from the secret police, who then arrested their parents as former *kulaks*—wealthy peasants.

Duty pulled her from her tears.

She walked into the clearing and the bird flew away.

A single brazen feather waited on the sandy earth. It glittered like fire. With magic.

She stuck the feather in her skirt pocket and Zoya led the way homeward.

They reached the partisan camp buried deep in the forest and invisible from the air. Nazi patrols feared to hunt here as the partisan territory grew every day.

Vasy led Zoya past green and brown tents scattered between low timber shelters covered with grass.

She smelt smoke and cooking. Her stomach gurgled. But food must wait. Anyway, not everyone liked the smell of goat at meals—just the taste.

Most partisans were locals from Byelorussia, but there were Ukrainian refugees like herself and Red Army survivors of the fascist invasion.

And, there were the Communist Party officials—bullies she tried to avoid.

But she needed to face Commander Yuri Bogomolov. He would know why the invaders were building the bridge.

She found the unit leader in the underground shelter used to control operations. He was beetroot-red from shouting orders.

"I need radio communication restored—no excuses. We're not using runners again. What will my superiors do if we go silent? They'll accuse us of being disloyal to Comrade Stalin. 'Not one step back', were his orders."

*But how perfect is our leader*, thought Vasy, not daring to speak her mind as her parents had done. Bullies had forced them from their home when Mama and Papa said the famine was deliberate. *Vasy, stop there. Just report. When I'm noticed.*

She felt worthless and was tempted to leave. Adults held more pressing concerns than a girl with goats.

As the Nazi vipers believed.

Bogomolov's bulk and gestures forced every command. Or was it his threats?

She had learnt 'to toe the party line'. She had become invisible.

"What does our little blonde *kulak* want?"

She ignored the insult. Even if the government prohibited owning property, the memory of her family's small farm made her stand tall.

For now, her report mattered more.

"The fascists are building a bridge across the Berezina. I counted fifty men and at least six tanks visible under the trees." He said nothing, so she asked, "What does it mean, Comrade Commander?"

"Nothing my force can't handle. *Kulak*, forget this. Time to tend your herd."

Dismissed. But she wouldn't forget the incident.

On the edge of the camp, beside her tiny tent, she found Zoya and her family dozing off. They didn't judge her like Bogomolov and mean adults.

"He ignored what we saw, Zoya. I'm just a child. Scum. Why am I here?"

"To brighten our lives." Vasy turned and smiled at Galina Sokolov, the woman who had rescued her and Kalyna. "You are better than Yuri and his lackeys. They don't see your true worth, *zolotyy*."

A frightened 'golden one'.

"If he ignores what I saw, we'll be in danger. What then?"

"He no longer acts alone. The Party has given others power—like Commissar Krupin. Tomorrow, Yuri will decide he has a superior plan—"

"—and he'll still ignore me."

"Better ignored than injured. You must come and eat. And distract us with another story."

Vasy followed Galina to the central firepit where the partisans ate and talked. Smoke, soup, and chatter curled around her. Her mind searched for a tale she hadn't told them.

In her skirt pocket, her fingers brushed the feather. Only one fable felt right. The origin of *Zharptica*—the Firebird.

Haggard faces gathered around her. Word had spread that she would weave her magic again.

Serious men, cunning women, and admiring youngsters stared at her, eagerly.

She was not *kulak* scum tonight.

"You remember The Firebird and Princess Vasilisa—"

"—you told that last week." A sandy-haired boy her own age groaned. "You have to know another. Why don't you?"

"I haven't told you who *Zharptica* is."

"It's a bird of ill omen," said one of Commissar Krupin's gang.

"Only if you're the Tsar and driven by greed and ambition. Only evil is punished. We aren't like that, are we?"

A chorus of voices replied, "Never."

Vasy nodded and raised her hands, palms down to settle them.

"You all know *Zharptica* comes from a distant land as a blessing for those in need. But what was the Firebird's origin?"

"A magician," said a young soldier clutching his ancient rifle.

She smiled. "Someone knows then, but I suspect not everyone. According to folklore, the Firebird is very rare, with plumage blazing red, orange, and yellow like the flames of a flickering fire. When removed, the feathers continue to glow. That is why some people try catching *Zharptica*."

She paused and studied her spellbound audience.

"Once upon a time, thousands of years ago, a meek and gentle orphan girl named Maryushka lived in a small village. People came from everywhere to buy her needlecraft. Many merchants asked her to move and work for them."

Vasy changed her voice to sound like her heroine and held out her hands. "'I will sell my embroidery to anyone who finds my work beautiful, but I will never leave this village where I was born.'"

Vasy paused, letting her words sink in.

"One day, the evil sorcerer Kaschei the Immortal heard of Maryushka's beautiful needlework. He turned himself into a handsome young man and visited her. Upon seeing her skill, he became angry. A mere mortal could not produce finer work than he owned."

She switched her voice again, making it sound deeper and darker. "'I will make you Queen of this realm if you will embroider for me alone.'"

"'I'm grateful and humbled by your offer. But I must decline. I never want to leave this village. I am sorry.'"

"This wound to Kaschei's pride sparked his magic."

Vasy drew invisible threads in the air.

"The evil sorcerer turned Maryushka into a flaming bird. *Zharptica*. He became a great black Falcon and picked her up in his claws."

Vasy flapped her arms like a bird as her words flew across the gathering.

"He stole Firebird Maryushka away from her village. To leave a memory of herself with her people forever, she shed her feathers onto the land below. As the last feather fell, she died in the falcon's talons."

Vasy's head dropped onto her chest. Silent and still as the crowd gasped. Then, she raised her head and stood, the *Zharptica* feather in her outstretched fingers. Moonbeams danced along its brazen edges.

"To this day, the glowing feathers are magic and remain bright. However, they show their rainbow colours only to those who love beauty and seek to make beauty for others. Together we can create the Firebird's world."

The hush turned to clapping, smiles, cheers, and nodding heads. Hands grasped her. Patted her on the back. Some even hugged her. The few brave ones stroked her magic feather.

"Next time," she said. "I would like someone else to tell a story. Others will have heard different tales. Stories must inspire us forever."

People agreed, then walked to the firepit's warmth or to the shelter of sleep.

Galina clasped her hands, grinning but serious as she said, "You sound as if you are leaving. Where to?"

"Wherever this Firebird feather takes me. Aren't we all dreaming of a journey?"

They strolled over to the edge of the encampment, arm in arm.

"One day, leaving might be vital to our survival," said the special woman who had taken her in.

"After this war? Life is meant to be better—brighter."

Galina trembled, so Vasy leant closer to catch her reply.

"People like the Tsar and Kaschei will continue to make rules and control us. I'm proud to be Ukrainian.

We're both survivors, me from the state's famine, the Holodomor. You and your sister from Stalin's Purge. Those that call you *kulak* will never give you freedom. Escape."

The warning words frightened Vasy. Her heart thumped. Her limbs grew weak. Galina hugged her. Stroked her hair and cheek.

"Where? What happens to you? My goats? We can escape together."

"Together would be dangerous. Maybe I can create a plan. Some friends left years ago for a land to the west with forests, snow, rivers, and freedom. Now sleep and dream, but don't be afraid."

Vasy fought her tossing mind and body. She slept and dreamt of escaping on the back of *Zharptica*. Unafraid.

Not until she was awoken by someone shaking her—roughly. Fingers dug into her shoulder and orders into her head.

"Get up. At once. The Commander and Commissar want to see you—immediately."

The harshness screamed traitor. Had someone reported every disloyal word shared with Galina?

Her fear grew as she trudged with the armed guards to the command shelter.

Commander Bogomolov and Commissar Krupin were with their three company officers, leaning over a map table.

"When the fascists retreat from Mogilev," said Bogomolov, "they will fall back to Minsk, fighting our Red Army in front and us in their rear—"

"—though, they'll need to cross the Berezina River," added Krupin.

Everyone ignored her, and the guards forced her into a corner.

"How can we trust our *kulak* goatherd?" asked Bogomolov. "Nobody else saw any enemy build-up in that area."

Krupin turned and pointed to her. "Not the most reliable spy. But in case there is a new bridge, it's our duty to stop the Nazis using it."

One officer stabbed at areas of the map. "Our forces are stretched, Comrade Leaders. We risk too much when other attacks are planned on their supply lines."

"Why not radio for an artillery strike on their camp—or bombers?" asked another officer.

"I can't. Some idiot failed to keep our radios working," said Bogomolov. "That's why you need to prove what you saw, little *kulak*." He waved her over. "As you spotted the fascists, you will take a message to our forces to the east and tell them what you found."

Vasy swallowed as she studied the map. Her dream of magical adventure dissolved.

"Across the front line? Alone?" she said.

"Exactly. Unless you were seeing more folk fantasies. The sooner you leave, the sooner that bridge is destroyed. You are dismissed."

"I'll provide you with a pass to get you through Soviet lines to my superior," said Commissar Krupin, "Convince him and return, *kulak*."

She returned to her tent where Galina waited.

"I have to report what I saw at the bridge to the Red Army leaders. I must make them believe me. Then come back."

"Don't. Find Kalyna and stay with her. You should be together."

Vasy wanted to be with her sister, but her heart was torn. She couldn't lose another mother.

"What about you? You're family too."

"I'm a survivor, remember. Your goats can stay with me. Just take Zoya. My love and strength to Kalyna when you find her. You are both in here."

Galina clasped a hand to her heart, then wrapped

her arms around Vasy. The long embrace ended too soon.

"Go, my brave girl. Fight and survive, *zolotyy*."

The tears for her second mother would come—after she grabbed food for the journey. Black rye bread, hard cheese, and raw red cabbage.

Goat's milk was also refreshing and valuable.

Zoya would be her sole companion for the journey. A young girl with a goat would not attract suspicion.

Not for the miles of forest they covered that morning and into the afternoon. The Nazi patrols were easy to avoid. They were wary of the partisan-controlled forest paths.

From the sound of gunfire, Vasy knew the front drew nearer. She must stay in the shadows, especially when the fields replaced the trees.

Burnt-out homes and dead bodies warned her to remain alert. How was she to cross the Dnepr River which the fascists were fighting to hold?

An easy night crossing for Kalyna, since she had a plane. Vasy only possessed a feather.

An abandoned village offered shelter while the sun set.

But a three-man German patrol emerged from the ruins, wielding guns and shouting at her. She didn't understand the words, but the meaning was clear from their gestures.

Who was she? Why was she here?

Vasy made a sad face. She pointed at the burnt-out buildings as if one had been her home. Then Zoya bleated, so Vasy touched the goat's udders. She pretended to milk her, then offer them a drink.

The soldiers grinned and nodded.

A shared bowl of fresh milk distracted the enemy. They left her to mourn in the ruins. Except, she planned her river crossing instead.

The moon and stars lit her search of the twisting

riverbank. No boats or even logs. Tired and frustrated, she was ready to fall asleep there on the damp ground.

The planes drew her attention first. Whispering through the air. Soviet biplanes. Night Witches flying east after a raid. One could be her sister. She noted where they seemed to land. That was her journey's end now.

Then, she heard voices—on the eastern bank. Speaking Russian.

She called out in a friendly voice.

"Please, can you help two lost partisans cross the Dnepr? We have fresh milk."

Frenetic whispers led to an answer.

"For the Motherland, yes. But what are your names? You sound young."

"Not too young to fight for freedom. We're Vasilisa and Zoya Chayka. Our sister flies with the 46th Taman Guards—*Nochnye Vedmy.*"

Cheers rang for the Night Witches.

Splashing in the glistening river followed. A soldier in strange balloon trousers appeared.

"I've brought you both floating devices like mine." He stared at Vasy. "Where's your partisan sister?"

She pointed to Zoya. "She's adept at fooling fascists."

He laughed, then helped attach the trousers on the curious goat.

Once across, Vasy told the Russian soldiers her mission. She asked if the 46th were nearby.

"Our nearest commander is there," said the platoon leader. "As part of our Air Army, she will pass the information on—or act."

One soldier offered to escort Vasy—once they had milk and breakfast.

Half-an-hour later, they reached a forest clearing.

Open-cockpit biplanes were parked around the edge. Female mechanics quietly tapped their wrenches, so as not to disturb their aircrews. The pilots and navigators slept under their planes' wings.

Vasy was tempted to find her sister. Warmth flooded her body, and she whistled their favourite folk song. They had so much to share, but duty came first.

She went to see the regiment's commander, Yevdokia Bershanskaya, and told her Kalyna Chayka was her older sister.

"One of our most fearless pilots," said the dark-haired Bershanskaya. "Sometimes I fear she takes too many risks. Perhaps as an all-female regiment we take risks to prove ourselves. What brings you here?"

Vasy explained about the bridge over the Berezina River and the enemy forces gathering there.

"Our radios are broken, so my commander ordered me to inform his superiors. I must find them."

"I will send that information. Stay with us. If we are ordered to raid that enemy base, we will need you. Meanwhile, spend time with Kalyna. She flies tonight."

Vasy searched the clearing for her sister.

Word had already reached Kalyna that her sibling was in the camp. She plucked Vasy from the ground and whirled her around. Zoya bleated and skipped around them.

"I never dreamt we would be together until this horrific war ends."

"Nor I. Strangely, I saw a fascist build-up that my commander ordered me to report. I've done that. Now I want to be with you."

Kalyna took her hand and led her to a tent where other women ate and drank. No haggard faces, just laughter and chatter. Even flowers sat on the tables, adding to the tempting smells.

"These are my flying sisters. You'll love them. We're living like gypsies now, moving from clearing to clearing as the army pushes forward. Temporary camps for a day or two. New targets every night. Wherever we are needed."

Most of the women were young. And there were not just Russians but Belarusians, Ukrainians, Cossacks, Tatars, and a Kazakh. Here was the wealth of the Motherland.

When one woman hugged her, Kalyna said, "This Ukrainian sister is my navigator, Irenka Gorecki."

Vasy embraced the navigator, her face brushing hair as brown as Kalyna's.

"At least we won't be moving until the main attack starts," said Kalyna. "We've been here for two days already, flying eight raids every night."

"I might have seen you returning last night. I was trying to cross the Dnepr."

"You crossed through fascist lines?" asked Irenka. "How?"

"With my goat Zoya's help."

A small face nudged her knee, and she gave Zoya a slice of cabbage. Nobody seemed to mind her faithful companion—unlike in the partisan camp.

Vasy let the chatter wash over her, relaxing in the warmth of this new family.

"Time to show you our Polikarpov U-2, our faithful *Zharptica*," said her sister.

"You remembered our dream." Vasy produced the feather. "I only have this to guide me."

Her sister stroked the feather. "Beautiful. A rainbow. Come and see ours, *zolotyy*."

Kalyna and Irenka's *Zharptica* was not just any wood-and-canvas biplane. A fiery red, yellow, and orange Firebird adorned both sides.

"We scrounged and made the right paint for our Po-2's masterpiece."

"Although it took months to complete," said Irenka. "Kalyna wanted it perfect."

"The Firebird inspires me to stay alive. To survive,

as we've both done—"

"With Galina's help," said Vasy. "She sends her love—and promises to keep fighting for freedom."

Nightfall approached, and the crew left to learn about their next target. Vasy stared at the fragile plane and realised the bravery of these women.

She hugged her sister when she returned for the missions ahead. Raids on enemy positions. Real danger.

The forest runway was too short for normal take-offs. So, the ground crews held the planes as their pilots built up speed. When the pilots signalled, the Po-2s leapt forward into the night, one by one.

Vasy couldn't sleep. She sat up all night with Kalyna's ground crew, waiting, praying, and biting her nails, even when the plane returned safely.

But the crew refuelled and rearmed the plane. Kalyna and Irenka made seven more raids.

By daybreak, Vasy had learnt what these Night Witches lived through.

Bershanskaya was there all night, concerned for her family. In the morning, when the last Po-2 was home, she approached Vasy.

"Command radioed back. The bridge must stay intact. We need it for our main attack. We must stop the Nazis using or destroying it. Tonight, three of our planes will bomb that camp. One will be your sibling."

"As my sister brought the information, I will lead," said Kalyna. "If she agrees."

Vasy agreed. "I'll show your navigators where the vipers are."

Except, she hesitated. She could find the bridge on the ground or on the map. But providing landmarks visible from the air?

Could she give them enough? Her sister and the others could die by her mistakes.

Attempting to sleep during the day, under a wing

with Kalyna, fear disturbed her. To one side, Irenka tossed, too. Was she also afraid?

Kalyna whispered to Vasy. "You're worried for us. Don't be. We'll find that camp and bring terror to the fascists."

"I want you to be safe. Those stories we created as children felt so real. Some still do. Like the Firebird. Does she always triumph? Or only at a price—her death?"

Her sister rolled closer and held her tight. "We're not paying that price. Our dreams will win. That's what helps me—us—survive. The Firebird can triumph, but it's never easy in this world." She searched Vasy's eyes. "Someone has hurt you. I can sense the pain."

The tears and the words were ready. "Partisan comrades who believe I am *kulak* scum, like my commandant and commissar. I'm not going back." Vasy hesitated before adding. "Galina told me to escape without her, but with you. West somewhere."

Kalyna rolled on her back, staring up at the wing. "Freedom. Mama and Papa's dream. We should fight for it. Although, I fear not. Some male officers in other regiments call me scum. I risk my life for the Motherland—as do you. Maybe it's time."

"For what? You have a plan? For when?"

Her sibling turned over and held her face in her hands. "Trust me. First, we sleep. Second, I attack those invaders. Then, we disappear. Patience, *zolotyy*."

Sleep came against the sound of mechanical woodpeckers—mechanics repairing aircraft. She dreamt she flew on the back of the Firebird with her sister.

A nose awoke her, and the tangy odour of goat.

"I found her something to eat." Kalyna's chief mechanic smiled at her. "I grew up tending goats. None as clever as—"

"—Zoya. I brought her into the world hence her

name 'life'. Where's my sister?"

The mechanic's face darkened. "In the medical tent. Irenka awoke with a fever. She was wounded yesterday."

Irenka had tossed in her sleep from pain not from fear.

"Who will navigate for my sister tonight?"

"The commander will decide. Talk to her."

Vasy ran to the command tent. The air crews were gathered with Bershanskaya around a map.

"Perfect," said the commander. "Please, come in. We need your help. Where are these fascists camped?"

Vasy pointed at where the bridge was being built on the partisan operations map.

"I can't describe any useful landmarks. I've never flown, except in my dreams on the *Zharptica*."

Bershanskaya chuckled. "Like on your sister's plane. A good omen for tonight."

Vasy turned to her sister. "With Irenka wounded, you haven't got a navigator."

"I'll follow the river. There's an unusual bend nearby on the map."

"I can fly with you."

The words were out. Not thought through. Just gut reaction. Her fear of flying and authority were dissolving.

"But I'm not trained," she added.

Bershanskaya stared at her. "That is correct. It takes months. You have three hours. We're breaking every rule here." She turned to the regiment's Commissar. "Will the Party condemn us if the enemy is stopped?"

The older woman studied the keen faces. "Unacceptable. I could have you all shot—if our brave sisters don't get killed." She paused and walked up to Bershanskaya. "This never happened. I wasn't here. I didn't allow fearless Navigator Vasilisa Chayka to fly tonight." She turned at the tent's opening. "Sisters, create more legends."

Vasy see-sawed between excitement and fear as she spent a tense three hours learning what she could from the real navigators. Gathered around Irenka's cot, they encouraged her, especially the two flying in the other planes.

When the others left for the night's missions, Kalyna knelt and whispered to Irenka.

"You'll always be my Hero of the Soviet Union. We have survived together, had fun together, and will always be family. Stay safe, my bravest friend."

Tears filled Irenka's eyes, so Vasy knew this was farewell.

Walking to the Po-2 in silence, Kalyna kept stopping to smile or hug her friends. The longest embraces were for her ground crew.

Vasy hugged Zoya. "You will be in safe hands."

She climbed into the *Zharptica*. It felt strange and yet familiar. Her sister's world.

She leant over Kalyna and stuck the precious feather above the instrument panel.

She'd returned the stolen feather.

Then, the roar of the engine. The wind rushing past her goggled face. Through the wires. Lifting the plane into the starry night-sky. Over the forest. Above her world. Across the Dnepr. Heading west.

How was she to navigate for Kalyna?

She leaned over the side of the Po-2. The ground threatened to pull her out and down—to her death.

She rejected the stupid threat as she gazed at her land's beauty from Kalyna's world. From *Zharptica's* realm.

The features below were familiar. She could find the bridge.

"Keep on this heading west, Kalyna. We can take down the tyrants. This is our challenge to their cruel rules. I was born to fly with you."

"We were born to fly together—with *Zharptica*."

Fields, villages, and forest sped past as the wind whispered. Then, the Berezina River glistened under the moon and stars like a sparkling snake. Coiling across the Motherland. Twisting around that bend towards the camp.

"Down. Ahead."

Kalyna wiggled the Po-2's wings for her sister pilots, then slowed the engine as they neared the target. The wind whistled past creating the sound of their broomstick. The witches were coming for the fascist soldiers—*Nachthexen.*

They glided to the bomb release point with only wind noise left to reveal their location.

"Now," said her sibling as tanks appeared below. Vasy released their two bombs. The plane shot up and safely away.

They returned three more times to awaken the viper's nest and create chaos.

On the final run, as the bombs dropped, machine-gun fire shot past, ripping into the canvas wings. Flames started on the tips.

Ash falling like feathers. Dropping towards the earth.

Behind more explosions as the two other Witches found their wrecked target. Sisters who escaped the bullets and headed home.

Unlike *Zharptica.* Fire was eating them. Heat blazing red, orange, and yellow like the sun. Burning them.

Scorching Vasy's face. She struggled to breathe. She tensed.

Yet, Kalyna kept flying westwards. Twisting *Zharptica.* Spinning her.

Wind ate the flickering flames. Devoured them. Sparks fell like glowing feathers onto the land below.

"Reborn from the fire," said Vasy. "Can we fly forever?"

"Our sisters will believe the flames killed us," said Kalyna, grief choking her voice. "However, we can fly further, wherever this *Zharptica* feather takes us. Family is life."

Tears came as Vasy replied, "A long voyage lies ahead. Head west—for forests, snow, rivers, and freedom. Our dreams of the Firebird's world will keep us alive. We're survivors."

The End


After diverse careers, Roland Clarke was an equestrian journalist and green activist when chronic illness hastened retirement. But he hasn't stopped exploring rabbit holes and writing - mainly mystery novels and varied shorts. Roland and his wife – both avid gamers - now live in Idaho (USA) with their four fur-babies, although their hearts remain in North Wales (UK).
www.rolandclarke.com
www.facebook.com/rolandclarkewriter
www.twitter.com/rrclarke53

# The Orchard
## By Beth Anderson Schuck

The April air sat heavy. It felt as damp as rain despite the sunshine slipping through the trees. Her tiny frame tensed from the effort as she dragged the axes behind her. The ax blades dug up vibrant green shoots of grass.

"Where are you headed so late, Miss Nels? It's almost supper," I added, hoping to spark interest.

Nels' shoulders sank as she dropped the axes on the ground. Her body dripped with disdain for whoever bothered her now. I could tell the sting of the community meeting was still fresh in her mind. Tears had soaked the front of her chambray shirt, mixing with sweat. Her cheeks were striped with pale skin among the dirt and pollen that caked her face and arms.

"I've got to cut out an apple tree or two. I'm behind schedule and spring is passing fast," Nels said. Her strong tone gave the impression she believed she could take down the trees by herself. I wasn't sure.

"Would you like some help?" I wanted to reassure her that she wasn't alone in this remote Utah community. I understood isolation. People who didn't really trust you nor really want you here, it seemed.

"No. I can do it. I mean, no ma'am."

"You can call me Della. I'm old enough to be a ma'am but prefer my name. It's less formal."

Nels nodded. She turned and picked up the heavy axes. A burlap bag strung over her shoulder added some bulk to her baggy denim overalls, at least one size too large for her wiry eleven-year-old frame.

A breeze began by the creek, rustling the leaves

up and out, spreading quickly. It reminded me of warm milk streaming over a wooden spoon.

"I think it's going to storm," I yelled after Nels. No response. "Be careful," I added. I sounded just like a mother despite my weak feminine aura.

I made a simple supper, not my favorite part of the day. On Saturdays, it was my turn to cook extra for Nels. The families of Junction, Utah made this agreement to share the work. The orchardist gets to stay in the barn, gets meals prepared by a different family each day, and gets a share of the profits from the sale of the fruit harvest. *If there is any. Profit, not fruit.*

I decided to scrutinize for myself how the orchard was progressing. At the community meeting, Mrs. Wills and Mrs. Swenson stated the trees weren't doing well since Nels' father had passed last winter. I had argued that it was too early to dismiss her (their idea). In my typical overly strong response, I stated emphatically that the trees looked healthier than ever.

Choosing a tree by the edge of the Empire apple grove—my favorite of all the apples—I leaned against the sturdy trunk, my tall frame almost meeting the tree branches, my head fitting between them. Nels had laid out her tools and now checked her notebook. She carried that journal everywhere, her nose in it often.

She readied herself, balancing her body weight back on her heels. Nels swung the ax and a *whack* rang out in the orchard. The wind whistled in my ears and the pine trees amplified the sound. It seemed almost musical. I swayed awkwardly with the wind.

After a few swings of the ax, Nels stopped to rest. She cocked her head and wiped her brow with her sleeve, pushing her short bangs straight up in the process.

*That girl needs a bath,* I thought. Just then Nels

startled and almost fell over backward.

I heard a moaning sound: *noooooooo...* It seemed to be the wind again and I glanced at the darkening sky. Storms were definitely coming.

Nels picked up the ax and began another swing, when *boom!* Lightning flashed and thunder clapped loud and close. I flinched and bumped my head on a tree branch. Ow, that was close.

"Nels, let's go," I yelled. I picked up the hem of my long skirt to make running possible. Turning to tear toward the barn, the nearest shelter, I glanced back at the girl. She seemed frozen. *Had she been struck by lightning?* Sheets of rain fell as dark clouds moved over the sun and surrounded the trees.

Nels put her face up to the sky to face the torrent. She howled, sounding more like a coyote than a human.

"*Owwooo*, don't tell me what to do!"

She slung the burlap sack over her shoulder and picked up the axes, one in each hand.

The rain let loose and pelted the tops of the trees, knocking some of the pink apple blossoms onto the ground.

The barn door creaked as I slid it open, startling Maisy the cow and Junior the donkey. They peered at me and then resumed munching their hay.

Nels' possessions were all in one corner of the barn. A feather pillow, flattened from use, and a small quilt that seemed toddler-sized, not nearly big enough for a young girl. Pens and inkwells sat dangerously on a crude wooden shelf hung by two rusty nails.

Her tools were impressive. Oil cans, rags, many sizes and types of saws, axes, and a ladder all lined up by the barn wall. Ropes, ties, and netting were arranged in a row outlining a space within the large barn.

"Did you hear that? That sound?" Nels asked, out

of breath from running with the heavy axes. Water dripped from her braids and down her nose.

"What, the thunder?" I asked, watching the water droplets pool on the dirt in front of me.

"No, no, the wailing. I think it was the trees." Nels' voice rose as the rain pounded the barn roof. "I think THEY made the storm to keep me from chopping that tree. Papa told me they spoke to him. The trees, I mean."

Nels' face began to register that her strange words sounded rather unbelievable.

I realized I was frowning. Shifting my weight allowed me to reset myself.

"You didn't hear it, did you?" she asked.

I shook my head. Then I remembered the moaning sound from the pine trees. "Well, I did hear the wind, right before the lightning."

Nels looked at the ground and kicked the dirt.

"I better dry off the tools before they rust. I'll need a fire to dry my clothes."

"Let me help," I said, feeling guilty for not supporting her notion of talking trees. I piled up the kindling in the fire ring and looked for the matches. Wanting to pull her out of her thoughts, I asked her about her papa.

"Does that journal help you to care for the trees?"

Nels pursed her lips. "Yes, Papa wrote everything down. He was always saying that he knew how to get nature on his side. Of course, that didn't help him during the flood," she added. She cast her gaze toward the ground and then even deeper down.

The December flood had damaged the orchards, washed away one house, and cost Nels' father his life. They never found his body.

"So, your papa talks to you in the journal?" I asked. "He's helping you with his words." I hoped to get a response.

Nels shrugged.

"I'm glad you'll be staying in Junction. I think we can help each other. I don't have many to talk to, except for the occasional visitor."

The ladies of Junction didn't appreciate strangers, so if anyone passed through, I was the only option for lodging. Meeting new folks was a task I enjoyed. I saw it as a distraction from my lonely existence in the isolated community.

Nels examined me from toe to head, looking for something. I wasn't sure what.

"I mean, living here is fine. I could use someone to really talk to," I stammered. I nervously picked at the kindling to stir up the fire and get it going.

Nels stripped off her wet overalls and shirt and picked up an equally dirty denim shirt and men's pants. She pulled on a belt and stretched it tight around her small waist. I wasn't sure it would hold up those ill-fitting pants.

She had no manners, really, but what did it matter if she was alone all the time? She draped her wet clothes over the only chair in the barn and pulled it close to the fire.

"So, you thought the trees were talking?" I said, settling in by the fire. The hem of my skirt was wet and heavy, so I held it close to the flames. The fire cracked and popped loudly. My body felt invigorated from the fire's heat and brazen noises.

Nels searched my face. She picked up the journal. "Let me read you something," she said. "It's dated January 1909. 'The trees are speaking to me again. They are telling me where to plant the new twigs brought from Oregon. When I am alone in the orchard, I listen. I hear them and do what they say.'"

I shuddered involuntarily and then searched for words.

"Nels, do you hear the trees, too?" I asked. I wasn't

sure I wanted to know, but it seemed like the right thing to ask.

Looking up from the journal, she closed it and set it on the shelf.

"Yes, I can." It was the last thing she uttered the rest of the evening.

\* \* \*

After the rains, it was damp and steamy as I rose early to start on the chores. Before the light completely broke, I saw a doe and two fawns walking by the creek. The mama's ears twitched. She turned her head toward me, scanning for potential danger.

"If only Nels had someone to watch over her," I said.

The doe stared at me and seemed to nod her head as she nudged her fawns onward. Urging them away from me.

I walked to the barn to let the animals into the corral, a chore assigned to me, as I don't have children to tend to in the morning nor a husband to worry me. Another way I'm separated from the women. Being thirty and unmarried in 1910 is rare. Here in rural Utah, it is unheard of. Not admired, to say the least. As I often explain to my aunts in the letters I write to them, I just enjoy being alone in nature. I haven't found anyone to shift my view around.

I unlatched and opened the barn doors. Maisy and Junior looked up. "I'm here. Let's go, you two." I tugged on Junior's harness to get him going in the right direction. Maisy always followed dutifully, just as a female in Junction should.

A large black cat sat by Nels, flicking its tail back and forth.

"Now Mr. Heks, I need your help. Keep watch over my things. I need to work all day to catch up on what I missed yesterday. I can't let Mrs. Swenson win. She thinks I can't be an orchardist. You know I can, right

Mr. Heks?"

The cat purred loudly.

"That's right. You're on my side, you handsome cat."

"Good morning, Nels." She nodded at me and continued packing up ropes, saws, and supplies in a handcart. "Where you headed today?"

She hesitated. "I'm going to the Grimes Golden grove. Those apple trees are about to bud and I need to trim the dead branches, check the irrigation ditches, and top off all the trees. Should be back at dinner," she added.

Nels turned the handcart around to head out the main barn door and I saw my chance.

"Mind if I walk with you as far as the schoolhouse? I need to check on a few things." I tried to sound as friendly as possible.

"Yes. I mean no, I don't mind," said Nels.

"Good. The animals are set, so let's go. What's the cat's name again? He is so handsome."

"That's Mr. Heks. My papa named him. I think it means 'witch' in Norwegian."

"Oh, my. That is a great name for a black cat."

As we left the small gathering of homes that formed Junction, the conversation flowed more easily.

"All our names mean something. My name is pretty interesting. Della means 'noble' and Falk means 'falcon.' So, I'm a noble bird. That almost seems like a joke, given my current life." I laughed. I felt I was rambling and Nels not even listening.

She tilted her head and stopped the cart.

"I love your name," she said. "My name means something, too. When Papa came over from Norway, he picked the surname 'Lund' which means grove, as he knew he would be an orchardist. I'm not sure why I have a boy's name, Nels. I like it though."

"Maybe your mama named you," I said, hoping to

find out about Nels' family.

"Well, no. My mama died having me, so she never saw me." Nels paused and began walking again, pulling the cart and balancing all the implements atop it. She had a lot to manage, not just with the cart.

*Why did I pry, just when she was opening up to me?*

I let some time pass, as that always helps folks to relax and forget. Then, as we neared the turnoff for the schoolhouse, I decided the time was right.

"Nels, I thought about what you asked last night. About the trees talking to you. I think I did hear something unusual. I didn't recognize it, but it was musical, pulling me in to listen harder. Was that what you heard?"

"Miss Della, I don't know. I'm pretty sure I'm the only one who can hear them. I think I'm cursed or something. My papa could hear the trees, that I know. But why would I hear them? What good could come from it? Thanks for talking to me, but this is something I have to figure out for myself."

As Nels rolled the cart farther and farther down the path, I cursed myself for not knowing what to say or do for this girl. *If only I could make her realize she's not alone.*

\* \* \*

Since I am unmarried and not so odd as to scare children, the residents determined I should be the teacher. Junction was too far from anything that resembled civilization for the children to go elsewhere. The children did need to learn to read and write and a bit of history. I agreed, even though my temperament wasn't suited for the task. What I was suited for was yet to be determined.

As I looked over the dusty schoolroom, I realized there were ten desks and chairs along with the teacher's table. It was cramped. A more than adequate wood stove and plentiful windows created a home-like atmosphere. When classes began this fall, there would be ten children, six from the Swensons alone and four from the rest of the homes. If Nels joined, I would need another desk and chair.

"I will ask Mr. Swenson if he will make a desk and chair for Nels. He obviously loves children, and how could he refuse the new schoolmarm?" I said this to no one, but it seemed logical.

Nels could read well, but she needed to spend time with the other children. Her mature nature could help me with the young ones. I wasn't sure I could keep the children on task.

A group of ravens cawed loudly. The racket interrupted my thoughts. I stepped outside and locked the door. The children were not excited about starting school, so there was no risk anyone would bother the schoolhouse, but I wanted to appear responsible.

The ravens circled over the trees across the path. I had to see what interested them.

"Caw, caw, that's all you say. I need to know who is gnawing off these trees. Can't you tell me?"

It was Nels, of course. Talking to the universe, I guess.

On the ladder and balancing a saw, she gripped the top of a rather spindly apple tree. Her voice was loud above the trees and echoing off the tall canyon walls.

"Yes, I'll leave out some leftovers after dinner tonight. Mrs. Swenson's bread is always stale anyway. You can have it all."

Not wanting to be seen, I pretended to gather sticks for my wood stove. As I stuffed the sticks into my bag, I saw Nels clip off the top branches of the tree, sculpting it to a roundish shape resembling a dome.

"That didn't hurt, now did it?" she said. "You look much better."

*OWWW.*

I heard a low moaning, which sounded the same as Maisy when she doesn't want to go into the barn.

*OWWW.* I squatted down to see if I could hear better lower to the ground. I didn't want to disturb whatever was going on in the orchard.

Nels shouted, "You're fine. Your branches will grow stronger if I limit them. Trimming doesn't harm you, it helps."

*Caw, caw* rang out from the ravens again.

"I'm done. I need to go to the creek and then back to the barn. I'll be back next week. Please have your flowers out by then," she added.

*"Woooooo,"* was the mournful response.

I sat down on the grass and hid behind the tree trunk. Nels certainly talks to the trees, and I think they talk back. If it helps her, that shouldn't bother anyone. But I know the people of Junction don't like odd or different. Her rare talent needed to remain a secret.

Nels finished packing up the handcart and began to pull it out of the orchard.

I called to her, "Nels, wait for me."

She stopped and turned around. "Sure, but I'm headed to the creek to check on the irrigation tracks."

"Ok, I'll walk that way too. I'm getting the schoolhouse ready. I'm the teacher now and I want it to be organized the first day."

Nels nodded, but clearly wasn't interested.

"With the rest of the summer, I'm going to review history, so I can teach that too. Not just reading and penmanship."

"Papa loved stories and told me all about Norway's history."

"Could you tell me sometime? I'd love to know all

about it."

"Why?"

"Well, we need to understand the past to avoid making mistakes again and again. And I think it's interesting to learn about the past."

The ravens glided silently overhead.

"Are they following us?" I asked.

"Well, probably, Miss Della. I promised them some bread later."

I raised my eyebrows so she would explain.

"Well, the ravens promised to watch over the Grimes orchard and see what is eating the tree bark. If I feed them bread, they will scare off the animals for me. That way I won't have to put up fencing around the trees. The ravens will save me a mess of work."

I nodded; that made good sense. This girl was smart when it came to trees.

* * *

The last Saturday in August arrived. So, I invited myself over to the barn, also known as Nels' place, to share dinner. Beans with salt pork made an easy meal. With the last of the peaches, I made a cobbler. *Only one week until school begins.* I needed to convince Nels to join us. *Peach cobbler is so tasty. It makes a person malleable,* I reasoned.

I added a history book onto the wheelbarrow already piled high with food and plates for dinner. Reading aloud to Nels had made us closer. It was something she enjoyed. I did, too.

Mr. Heks sat by the barn, staring at the grasshoppers around him. We had a large invasion of grasshoppers this month, but Nels wasn't worried. *They feed the birds, which help my trees, so I'm not complaining about them,* she had told me.

The orchards had provided plenty of plums, peaches, and apples. Mrs. Swenson admitted that she was pleased with Nels' work, so the girl could stay another year. I had kept Nels' secrets. Luckily, the ladies of Junction didn't want to get to know her. They were happy to keep their distance. She could retain her peculiar ways, just as I kept mine.

"Nels, lets heat up these beans. Can you start a fire, please?"

Nels startled awake, as she had been napping. She sat up and carefully folded her quilt and set it on her pillow.

"Yes, ma'am," she said.

Mr. Heks followed me in. "I think he's hungry too. I know I am."

As Nels arranged the kindling into a tepee-like shape, the cat meowed.

"Don't worry, we'll have some for you." She patted his head. His tail swished back and forth. "Let's get this lit, so we can eat."

Soon the fire crackled, and I placed the cast iron pot of beans on the grate over the flames. We ate silently, except for the cat. He slurped up the beans with gusto. Everyone had their fill of beans and bread, so we decided to eat the cobbler later.

Pulling out the United States history volume, I asked where we had stopped reading last week.

"I think we're ready for Betsy Ross, isn't that right, Nels?"

"Yes."

She settled in with her elbows on her knees, leaning close to me.

Mr. Heks swished his tail in agreement. He sat too near the embers of the fire and a sharp odor filled the barn. His tail was singed—just enough to smell horrible, but not enough to hurt him.

"He's one fine cat, that one. Always follows you where you are working."

"He's my companion on my journey," said Nels.

"Speaking of friends, I want you to attend school

with me. You are smart and need to continue learning. Now that you are staying another year, let's try it." I paused and decided to let that stand as my request.

I waited for a response, a look, or any emotion. I couldn't read anything.

"I don't think so, Miss Della. I have a lot of work to do and the orchards are my duty." She stirred the fire with a poker. The cat skirted away as embers flared into flames.

"How about this? You can do both. I do reading in the morning. You can skip that and join us for afternoon classes. You'll be done by 3:00 p.m. and can work until dark. I need you to be there. You're so calm and helpful." I paused and convinced myself I could say what I most feared.

"I'm not sure I can teach the children without you." *There, I said it out loud.*

Nels glanced sideways without moving her head. "Well, maybe. I don't have anything to wear, though."

"Well, I thought of that. I made a pair of overalls out of denim from a lodger's pants that were left behind."

Nels smiled. "Oh my, Della, you've been planning this for a while."

I nodded. "We have to stick together. We're not like the others. But we can be close, a family of sorts. Looking out for each other. Being there for each other."

"Let me think on it," she said. "But for now, Mr. Heks and I need some of that cobbler."

* * *

The first day of school arrived with a stormy beginning. I stopped by the barn to remind Nels to meet us at the schoolhouse at noon, but she was already out working. I still managed to get to school early. I wasn't too wet, just a bit disheveled.

It was damp and a bit chilly, so I started a fire in

113

the woodstove. I wrote my name in large letters on the small chalkboard. A small stack of readers sat on the corner of the teacher table.

I heard the children before I saw them. Loud thumps as dirt clods were thrown at each other and at the trees. The girls squealed loudly and the boys guffawed.

*Oh my, I have my hands full.* I took a deep breath and stared at the floor. *You only need to appear confident. They will behave. Just demand it.*

"Let's go children," I yelled as I rang the bell that Mrs. Wells gave me. *Clang, clang.* It was time for school to begin.

The morning wasn't terrible. Well, not really. The boys had to sit on one side, as they could not stop teasing the youngest girl, Johanna. I was able to assess students' reading by asking them to read aloud from the Bible. Most of the children were assigned the level one reader.

"Let's break for lunch. Since it's wet outside, we will eat at our desks. If it clears up, we'll have a break at 1:30 p.m. to run around and work off some energy." Loud groans arose from the boys' side of the room, but they were hungry enough to ignore the hardship of staying inside a little longer.

I stepped outside to see if there was any sign of Nels. Still misting, the heavy air surrounded me. Everything outside was muffled, the trees blurry in the mist, and the sounds of the orchard swished through the wet leaves. Dusty-green evergreen trees and muted orange rock walls surrounded the tiny schoolhouse. Looking in every direction, I saw no one.

I ate my jelly bread quickly. I pulled the golden apple from my lunch bag. "These apples are the best of the year, so crisp." Nels was making this place livable with her tree magic. I placed the core back in my bag, for the donkey loves them.

"Let's begin this afternoon with history. Who can tell me the first US president?" No response or sign of life from the children.

"Who can name any US president? Can anyone recite the presidents with me? I'll start." I was desperate for a response.

I heard the *caw, caw* of the ravens.

I noticed the children straining in their seats. *Perhaps the questions are too difficult for the first day.* No, it was something going on outside.

"Miss Falk, look out the window," said one of the children.

I can only call what I saw a parade approaching the schoolhouse. A pair of ravens marched at the front of the procession, followed by Mr. Heks swishing his tail. Next came a family of skunks, alongside a doe and two fawns. Wrens and finches flitted above them, tweeting and singing a light song. Ground squirrels ran around in circles behind the deer but moved forward in step with the others. Butterflies and dragonflies zoomed up and down above Nels' head, sparkling like stars in the sunlight. Dressed in the new overalls I had made, she pushed her handcart full of tools, her hair flowing down her back. It had actually been brushed. Rays of sunshine hit the parade, lighting the entire scene from above.

"What is she doing, Miss Falk? Is she coming here?" Johanna asked.

"Yes. Nels will be joining us," I responded. I couldn't suppress the huge grin bursting through my "teacher" face.

"Why are the animals bringing her?" one of the older boys asked.

I cleared my throat, as it had tightened up with the excitement.

"She is friends with the animals. And with nature. They are supporting her on her journey. Her journey to be a part of Junction, just like the rest of us. You will like her, I'm sure of it."

Nels parked the handcart under the scrub oak tree by the schoolhouse. She waved goodbye to the animals. "Thanks for the escort. I can handle it from here."

The wind swept up from the creek and rustled through the orchard. The fresh scents of the earlier rain blew into the schoolhouse.

The children clapped their hands as the animals retreated back into the trees. Nels came through the door to the elation of the children.

She smiled at me and nodded. "I made it, Della. I mean, Miss Falk."

"Yes, you've arrived. Right where you need to be."

The End

Beth Anderson Schuck is a retired librarian who believe reading can take you anywhere. She writes historical fiction featuring willful female characters. Being in nature whether hiking, birdwatching or gardening makes her whole.
www.twitter.com/schuck_beth

# Simon Grey and the Yamamba
## By Charles Kowalski

**I** cried out in alarm.

This is not a very clever thing to do when you're traveling through a dangerous country, trying your best to avoid discovery. But it's hard not to do when you're walking down a forest road at dusk and just a few yards in front of your face, a small animal flies into the air.

To make matters worse, I involuntarily ducked behind Oyuki. I had been trying hard to make a good impression on her, hoping she would see me as a strong protector on the journey. But at the first sign of danger, I ran behind her like a child hiding behind his mother's skirt.

"Angels and ministers of grace, defend us!" I gasped in an attempt to redeem myself a little with the erudition I had gained at sea under a Shakespeare-loving captain. "What was that? Some new kind of yokai?"

Oyuki and I were both born with the ability to see the world of ghosts and spirits. This is an awful nuisance if you live in haunted London, so I had tried to escape by going to sea. A ship bound for Japan seemed most likely to offer a long voyage free from ghosts, so on that fateful day in 1620, I eagerly signed up as a cabin boy. But a shipwreck made me first a castaway and now a fugitive, as Oyuki and I made our furtive journey to the English trading post of Hirado with help from the *yokai*, the spirits that wandered around Japan by night.

In the twilight, we could see the animal above us. It was a fox. And it was not in fact flying but caught in a snare trap. It now dangled by a rope from a tall bamboo stalk, thrashing around in a vain attempt to free itself, yipping and barking madly.

"The poor thing," Oyuki said. "Let's get it down."

I grasped the bamboo and bent it until the fox was within Oyuki's reach. She took the fox gently in her arms and freed it from the rope. "*Yoshi, yoshi,*" she crooned, cuddling it and stroking it between its ears. "Are you hungry? I'm sorry we can't offer you your favorite fried tofu or *inari-zushi,* but at least we have plenty of cucumbers."

Taking the cue, I unslung my pack and took out a cucumber. Oyuki sat cradling the fox in her lap and fed it piece by piece. The fox ate voraciously and scampered away, pausing to look over its shoulder and give us one last bark that I took to mean "thank you."

We watched it out of sight before picking up our packs, and resumed our trek along the riverbank. Since we were fugitives from the Shogun, whose chief advisor held such an interest in our gift that he had imprisoned both of us in Edo Castle to discover our "secret," we stayed away from the well-traveled and patrolled Tokaido road. Instead, we followed rivers, guided at night by a froglike water sprite called a *kappa* whose fondness for cucumbers was the reason for our abundant supply of them.

As we walked, Oyuki, who was born in Japan, pointed out various sights, both to teach me Japanese and to help me understand this unique country. "That's a *torii,*" she would say, pointing to a wooden gate in the middle of the forest. "It's the entrance to a shrine to Inari, one of the eight million gods supposed to dwell everywhere in nature. And that..." she would say, pointing to a statue by a wayside temple, "is a Buddhist saint named Amida. People who believe in him hope to be reborn in a paradise called the Pure

Land."

I tried to wrap my mind around these names. For me, even with a clergyman father, I struggled to remember all the Twelve Apostles. I continually marveled at how the Japanese managed to keep all these heavenly beings straight.

As we walked, the sound of rushing water grew louder. Suddenly, the trail veered away from the river as the water cascaded into a narrow gorge between two high, sheer cliff faces. It was an awe-inspiring sight, but a formidable obstacle for us. Our yokai guide could probably navigate the river with no difficulty, but there was no space for us humans to walk between the rapids and the rocky walls.

As we stood there, wondering what to do, a faint sound reached my ears over the roaring of the falls. For a moment, I wondered whether something was wrong with my hearing, because in that desolate spot, I thought I heard the tinkling of a bell.

A moment later, we saw the source of the sound. Coming down the trail in the opposite direction was a monk in Buddhist robes and a broad-brimmed straw hat. The sound I had taken for a bell came from the metal rings at the tip of his wooden staff.

I panicked and resisted the urge to hide behind Oyuki again. Apart from the Shogun's guards, a monk was the last person I wanted to meet. I was dressed as a *bozu*, a young monk. The disguise had gotten us safely out of Edo, but any real monk would see right through it. I hastily put on my *takuhatsu-gasa*—a domed hat that concealed my foreign face—and tried to look pious.

"Hello!" the monk called to us. "Where are you headed?"

"That way," Oyuki answered vaguely. "Just wondering how to get to the other side of the gorge."

"This path takes you to the village," the monk

said, pointing back the way he had come. "But the little path that branches off to the right goes up the mountain and down the other side. You'll be able to pick up the river from there."

"Thanks!" said Oyuki.

The monk turned to go, but then paused. "I'd strongly urge you, though, to find lodgings in the village tonight and set off again in the morning. You don't want to be on the mountain after dark with the risk of running into a sudden storm—or worse, the *yamamba*."

Oyuki thanked him politely, and I heard the receding tinkle of the rings on his staff as he continued onward.

Once he was well on his way, I pushed back my hat. "What's a yamamba?" I asked Oyuki.

Instead of answering, she pointed at the monk's retreating figure. "Look."

I followed her point and noticed a bulge in the back of the monk's robe, right below his waist.

"What's that?" I said.

"I think it's a tail."

I turned and gave her an incredulous look. "What?"

"That monk is probably the fox we helped. Some foxes are messengers of Inari and have powerful magic. They can disguise themselves as other animals, or even humans, so well you'd never know—unless they forget themselves and show their tails."

She set off down the path, and I hastened to keep up with her. Soon, we came to a smaller path branching off to the right. Without hesitation, she turned onto it.

I stopped at the crossroads. "You're planning to climb the mountain?" I asked in disbelief.

"*Kitsunebi!*" Oyuki called.

A ball of blue fire materialized in front of her. This was the kitsunebi, another of our yokai guides, and it illuminated the path with a pale light. With its help, we had traveled by night and slept in secluded places by day. But even so, after the monk-or-possibly-fox's warning, the mountain path looked too dark and dangerous for my taste.

"What else would you have us do?" she said. "It's less risky to push on than to go where there are people who might report us to the Shogun's guards."

"What about the yamamba?" I called after her, still no closer to knowing what that meant. But she was already on her way.

Oyuki set a fast pace, even when climbing the steep slope, and I struggled to keep up with her. The kitsunebi, of course, followed her rather than me, and I had to hurry to stay within its circle of light if I wanted to see the rocks and tree roots underfoot before they could twist my ankles.

As we neared the summit, I heard an ominous rumble of thunder, soon followed by the patter of raindrops on the leaves overhead. Before long, the rain came down in torrents. Within minutes, my robes were completely soaked, and the rocks underfoot grew so slippery that even Oyuki slowed her pace to a crawl. Lightning flashed in the distance, followed a few seconds later by another thunderclap.

Oyuki stopped and turned to me, probably to confer about what we should do, and I wondered the same thing myself. We were so close to the top that it would take us almost as long to go down this side as the far side. Whether we chose to turn back, go on, or stay put and seek shelter, we were equally easy targets for lightning.

But her first question was, "Do you smell that?"

I could smell nothing but wet earth, wet wood, and wet cloth. But soon after she asked, a different, unexpected scent reached my nostrils.

"Wood smoke?" I said.

She nodded. "Where there's fire, there's bound to be life. Come on!"

We forged ahead, climbing our careful way over the slippery ground, until we reached what I dared to hope was the summit. To our right, a sheer cliff dropped to the river far below, and to our left, the possible source of the smoke: a small house made of wooden beams pushed into odd angles by time. The windows were shuttered against the storm, but under the broad eaves hung a red paper lantern, swaying wildly in the wind but still lit with a flickering light. It was the most welcome sight I could imagine.

As we stared in wonder, the door slid open. Behind it was an extremely old woman, her long, white hair unbound and unkempt, hastily adjusting her disheveled kimono. When she saw us, her eyes widened with understandable surprise.

"What in the world are you doing up here?" she said in a voice that sounded cracked and rusty from long disuse. "Come in before you get struck by lightning!"

We hurried through the door and stood on the packed-earth floor of the entryway, trying to wring as much water out of our clothes as possible. When we had gone from dripping to merely soaked, we stepped out of our sandals and up onto the *tatami* straw-mat floor of the living room. In the center, a fire burned in the open hearth, an iron pot hanging over it. The smell of stewed vegetables filled the room, making my stomach growl.

"Now, who might you be?" the old woman said. "And what are two children doing out here on their own?"

"My name is Oyuki, and this is Simon," Oyuki replied, deftly avoiding the second part of the question. "And you are?"

"Around these parts, they call me Hotchopa."

"Do you get many guests up here?" Oyuki said. "I wouldn't have imagined it was a very well-traveled road."

"Oh, you'd be surprised," she said. "I've had many weary travelers come in for supper. Of course, I wasn't expecting anyone on a night like this, but you came at the perfect time. I was just getting ready to give my old bones a soak in the bath, and then have some dinner. I hope you like *nanban-ni*."

"I don't think I've ever tried it," I said. "What is it?"

"*Ni* means 'stew'," Oyuki explained, "and *nanban* means...well, no offense, but 'southern barbarian', their term for Europeans. It's vegetables stewed in their idea of Western style, with fried onions and red peppers."

I had no energy to object. If Hotchopa wanted to serve us a hot meal, I was willing to forgive the name of the dish, for both the cultural snub and the shaky sense of direction.

"Here's the bath," Hotchopa said, sliding aside a door to a smaller room. In the center stood a wooden tub, resting on a metal pan atop a stone firebox with embers glowing inside.

Oyuki recoiled. For some reason I had yet to learn, she possessed a deep-seated fear of hot water. "Simon can go first," she said.

"Very well," Hotchopa replied. "Then you can come and help me in the kitchen."

I passed through the door. As soon as Hotchopa closed it behind me, I gratefully peeled off my sodden robes, gave myself a scrub with the bag of rice husks provided, and eased myself into the tub.

After coming in from the downpour, a bath felt like paradise. It was heated to Japanese temperature, though, meaning much hotter than I was used to in England. After a few minutes, I stood up, and was just about to climb out when the door slid open. I hastily sank back into the water as Hotchopa came in.

"I'll dry those by the fire for you," she said, gesturing to the robes. "How's the bath? A bit lukewarm, perhaps?"

"No, not at all," I said hurriedly. But she had already taken an armload of sticks from the stack in the corner, crouched by the bath, and started to feed them into the fire.

"I say, that's quite hot enough, thank you," I repeated. She ignored me and continued to throw fuel into the fire at an increasingly rapid rate.

"I think I'll get out now, actually," I said, squirming as steam began to rise from the surface of the water. "I wouldn't want to keep Oyuki waiting. Dinner must be ready by now."

Hotchopa finally raised her head to look at me, grinning from ear to ear—literally. Her mouth had become impossibly wide, and her lips drew back to reveal long, sharp fangs. Horns protruded from her forehead, and her eyes glowed red like live coals.

In a deeper and darker voice, she growled: "Not yet."

I screamed.

I tried to jump out of the bath, but before I could move a muscle, Hotchopa thrust a finger at me, the nail now a long, sharp talon.

"*Katamare!*" she said.

My body froze. I could still breathe and move my eyes, but everything below my neck was completely paralyzed. I sat helpless in the bath as the water grew hotter and the steam thickened.

Oyuki burst into the room, kitchen knife in hand. Hotchopa turned her demon face toward her. Oyuki stopped and drew back, her eyes and mouth wide. Then, the horror in her face gave way to steely resolve, and she charged, her knife hand upraised.

Hotchopa thrust a clawed hand at her. "*Katamare!*"

Instantly, Oyuki stopped in her tracks, the knife still held high in her hand.

"Yamamba," she said in a voice faint with fear, as comprehension dawned. "Short for *yama-uba*. Hag of the mountain."

Hotchopa glowered at her. "I don't much care for that word," she said. "Call me witch, crone, ogress... or the inventor of nanban-ni made with real nanban." She poked me with a nail, as though testing whether I was done. "This will be my first time to sample foreign food. I wonder how you'll taste?"

"Awful!" I shrieked. "Horrible! Ghastly! I'm English, and everyone knows English food is the worst in the world. Have you ever tried salt pork that's been sitting in a ship's hold for a year? That's been my diet."

"In that case," she said, reaching for a small clay pot on the shelf, "we might need a little extra miso."

"Hotchopa," Oyuki pleaded, "you were human once, right?"

"That I was."

"You were a mother? You had children?"

"That I did."

"Then, please! If you ever had a mother's heart, think of Simon's poor mother, on the far side of the world, waiting for him to come home. Could you really live with yourself if she never saw him again because of you?"

"Never saw him again?" Hotchopa snorted. "Some women have all the luck! I only wish my son had been lost at sea, never to be seen again, before he could do what he did to me!"

"What did he do?" I asked.

"You know what this place is?" Hotchopa demanded. "It's an *ubasuteyama*."

I had never heard the word before, but the way she almost spat it out sent a chill through me even as the water scalded me. It clearly held meaning for Oyuki, for her eyes widened in shock.

"Famine in the land," Hotchopa continued. "Not enough food for all the mewling brats he spawned with that wicked woman he married. So, what does she tell him to do? Take his aging mother, who by then couldn't even walk on her own, up the mountain... and leave her there to die!"

"How horrible!" Oyuki exclaimed.

"How sharper than a serpent's tooth it is to have a thankless child," I quoted, once more praying that Shakespearean eloquence would come to my rescue.

"Well said." Hotchopa's glowing eyes scrutinized me. "You say you have a mother who loves you, waiting for you in your home country?"

"Yes. Yes, I do."

She leaned over the wooden tub until her face was inches away from mine. "When she's old and bedridden, do you promise to feed her and care for her? Just as she did for you when you were a helpless little baby?"

"Yes," I screamed. "Yes! A thousand times yes."

Hotchopa sighed. "Well, I wouldn't be so heartless as to keep you from ever seeing her again. I'll let you go free."

"Thank you," I cried. "Thank you, thank you, thank you!"

"On one condition!" Hotchopa continued, raising a clawed finger. "Go down to the village. Your little friend will stay here with me. Find my son and come back with him—or that horrid wife of his, I don't care which. His name is Goemon, and he's a mender of paper screens and umbrellas. If you come back with him, he will be my dinner tomorrow night. If you come back without him, it will be you. If you don't come back..." She gestured toward Oyuki. "It will be her. But one way or another, tomorrow I will feast on human flesh! Do we have a deal?"

I opened my mouth, but no words came out.

Hotchopa seized another stick and prepared to throw it into the fire. "What's it to be? Do we have a deal?"

I let out a scream of pain, which sounded something like, "Yes!"

Hotchopa raised a hand. *"Tokihanatare!"*

At once, I could move again. With a speed I never knew I possessed, I jumped out of the bath. Oyuki shut her eyes as Hotchopa seized a bucket and doused me with cold water.

My skin, now bright red, stung all over when the water struck it. Now I had some idea how a boiled lobster must feel, and I vowed then and there never to eat one again.

"For tonight, you've been reprieved," Hotchopa said. "But tomorrow, you will be either my messenger or my main course."

\* \* \*

As soon as the sun rose, I headed back down the mountain. I followed the path into the village and among the few shops by the roadside, I soon found one with a paper umbrella hanging from the eaves.

I had no idea how to approach Goemon. What could I say? *Hello, Goemon! Remember your mother, whom you left in the mountains to starve to death? Well, guess what! She's become a yamamba, and she sent me to invite you to dinner...*

The door slid open. I hastily put my hat on and stood still as a statue. From somewhere within, I heard a babble of children's voices with their mother shouting over them.

"Oh!" Goemon exclaimed when he saw me. "Good morning, bozu! Out on *takuhatsu*, are you? Collecting donations for your temple? Just a moment." He came out of the shop and placed a coin in my palm.

"It's not much," he said, "but it's all I can spare." He leaned in closer and added in a voice heavy with sorrow, "And please say a prayer for the soul of my mother. May she be reborn in the Pure Land."

Goemon went back to his shop, leaving me even more at a loss than before. I could never imagine doing to my own mother what Goemon had done to his, and it chilled me to think the practice could be so commonplace that the mountain where these poor old women were taken even had a name. On the other hand, he had clearly carried a terrible burden of guilt ever since. No closer to knowing what to do, I still knew one thing for certain—I couldn't deliver him or his wife into the claws of the yamamba.

As I walked slowly down the street, deep in thought, the sharp smell of scorched soy sauce reached my nostrils. "Tofu!" a vendor called. "Fried tofu! Inari-zushi!"

I stopped, went over to the shop, and lifted my hat slightly to look over the offerings. I saw blocks of bean curd, some white and some grilled brown, and balls of vinegar-soaked rice wrapped in fried tofu skins.

"I'd like some inari-zushi, please," I said, struck by sudden inspiration. "As many as you can give me for this." I handed the vendor the coin I had received from Goemon.

As soon as I had the vinegared rice balls in hand, I headed out of the village and back the way Oyuki and I traveled the previous day, until I came to the torii gate that marked the entrance to the Inari shrine. It was so far from human habitation that I wondered who would go to the trouble of building and maintaining it—but, as I had learned from Oyuki, Shinto shrines appeared anywhere someone witnessed anything that inspired a sense of awe and wonder.

I passed under the torii gate and climbed a flight of rough-hewn, moss-covered stone steps to the shrine, a miniature wooden house atop a stone pedestal. It was barely bigger than a birdhouse, but apparently big enough to be a suitable dwelling place for a god. I unwrapped my package, laid a piece of inari-zushi on the steps, sat down beside it, and waited.

Time passed. I grew so hungry that the urge to eat one of the rice balls myself was overpowering. The restraint that I showed by sitting still and resisting temptation, if I may say so myself, would have done credit to a real monk.

It was late afternoon when I finally heard a rustling by the shrine entrance. I looked and saw a fox under the torii gate, sitting on its haunches and staring at me.

"Here, boy!" I called. "Come here, boy! I've got a treat for you!"

The fox continued to sit still and look at me through narrowed eyes.

I realized that I might have made a mistaken assumption. "Or are you a girl?" I tried. "Here, girl!"

The fox's eyes narrowed even further.

I made one final attempt. "O honorable messenger of the divine Inari," I said with a bow, "please deign to accept my humble offering."

The fox finally stood up, stretched, and climbed the steps to where I sat. I watched as it happily devoured the inari-zushi.

When it had consumed the first piece, I set out the second. As the fox tore into that one, I asked, "Are you the fox we helped out of the trap yesterday? The monk on the path who gave us directions—was that you?"

The fox stopped and looked up at me but made no move that I could take as either a confirmation or denial.

"Well, if it was, thank you," I said. "And I have just one more favor to ask." I told it the story of our encounter with the yamamba. "So, you see," I concluded, "either Goemon gets eaten, or his wife does, or Oyuki does, or I do. I'm trying to arrange things so that no one gets eaten. Will you help me?"

The fox looked up at me, licked its lips, and inclined its head.

\* \* \*

With the fox trotting along beside me, I went back to the village, and showed it where Goemon lived. The fox slunk around the back of the house and reappeared a few moments later.

"Do you think you can do it?" I asked.

The fox gave a bark of what I hoped was agreement, and we set off up the mountain.

When we reached the door of Hotchopa's hut, I turned toward the fox, but it was gone. In its place stood a man that anyone would have taken for Goemon.

The door slid open to reveal Hotchopa with knife in hand. She was in her old woman's guise, but as soon as she saw the replica of Goemon, she let out a scream of rage that echoed across the gorge and reverted to her red-eyed yamamba form.

"Goemon!" she shrieked. "How could you do such a thing to your own mother? I gave you life, and you took mine away!" She lunged with the knife, and the fox-as-Goemon stepped back, barely dodging the sharp blade.

Hotchopa leapt down and chased the fox outside, screaming curses and slashing with the knife after each. "I nourished you"—slash—"with my body! And now"—slash—"your body"—slash—"will nourish"—slash—"me!"

With a look of terror on its face, the false Goemon turned tail and ran. And unfortunately, that was true in every sense of the word. A fluffy, red, white-tipped tail peeked out above the waist of his trousers.

As soon as Hotchopa saw it, she unleashed another scream of rage, turned, and charged at me, her knife raised high. "Try to fool me, will you?" she shrieked. "You'll feed me instead!"

The knife bore down on me. My back to the precipice, I had nowhere to run.

A small red shape darted across the path in front of Hotchopa. I barely dodged out of the way as she tripped over the fox, stumbled, and pitched forward— over the edge of the cliff.

Her scream echoed from one side of the ravine to the other as she plummeted down to the rapids.

When the echoes died away and I could hear nothing from below but the sound of rushing water, I turned to the fox. "Thank you!" I said, giving it the last piece of inari-zushi.

As it ate, I went back into the house, automatically stepped out of my sandals, and ran through the house calling Oyuki's name.

"Here!" I heard her muffled voice. "Simon, I'm here!"

I traced the voice to the kitchen, coming from under a huge clay pickle jar. After trying unsuccessfully to lift it, I rocked it back and forth until I had moved it far enough and lifted the square of wooden floor underneath to reveal Oyuki. She took my hand in one of hers, putting the other on the edge of the hole, and with some difficulty, scrambled out.

"The yamamba?" she asked anxiously.

"She's gone." As I told her the story, we retrieved our bags, and I began searching from room to room, checking every box, drawer, jar, and loose floorboard I could find.

"Simon, what are you doing?" Oyuki demanded. "Let's get out of here! If being left in the mountains to starve didn't finish her off, the fall might not have either."

"In every story I've heard about witches who prey on unsuspecting travelers," I told her, "they've had some kind of treasure in the house."

"We have the greatest treasure of all," she said. "Our lives. Let's not push our luck."

I had to admit she had a point. We slung our packs over our shoulders and left the house.

The fox had finished its treat and gone its way. Oyuki summoned the kitsunebi and started down the descending path, but I paused for a moment at the edge of the cliff and listened. I still heard nothing except the roar of the river.

I set down my pack, pressed my palms together, closed my eyes, and turned my face heavenwards.

"May she be reborn in the Pure Land."

After a moment of silence, I picked up my pack again, and hurried to catch up with Oyuki.

The End

Charles Kowalski is the author of the Japan-themed Simon Grey middle-grade historical fantasy series. His thrillers for adults have won the Rocky Mountain Fiction Writers' Colorado Gold Award and been nominated for the Killer Nashville Silver Falchion Award and the Adventure Writers Grandmaster Award. He has lived in Japan for over 20 years.
www.facebook.com/SimonGreyYokai
www.twitter.com/SimonGreyYokai

# A World of Trouble
## By Rebecca Douglass

**M**y name is Mattie May Scott, and I am in a world of trouble.

I mutter the words under my breath while I'm standing ankle deep in water and trouble. Pretending this is a story makes it less scary. If things had gone the way I planned, it would be a story about running off on a lark to go to Conconully and see an aeroplane fly. Instead, it turns out to be about getting myself and my best friend into maybe more trouble than we know how to handle.

It's Daddy's fault for telling me about the aeroplane at the fair.

"Mattie! Stop woolgathering and grab ahold of this!" Gordon's shout yanks me right out of my thoughts and back to the trouble we're in. This is no story I'm making up. I shake my head to clear it and take a grip on the log Gordon's trying to move. After a glance at the rising water, I throw my back into the effort.

We had a pretty good time up until this rain started. We saw the aeroplane and no one caught us eating ice cream under the stands. Even the rain was okay until we left the road to try to save these cows that shouldn't have been out. Now the fight to save the Johansson's cattle is a fight to save our own lives, too. I wish I'd obeyed Daddy and stayed home to take care of the farm. I bet Gordon does, too, but I don't ask. We both need all our breath to clear this blockage in the creek before it floods the little hump of land we're sharing with a half a dozen cows and Gordon's horse, General.

*General.*

"Gordie!" I have to yell to be heard over the roar of the creek. The rain isn't beating on my hat anymore because I lost it somewhere in the mad scramble to get to high ground when the creek cut loose. Instead, water's running down my face, my hair plastered to my head. My braid is a wick that draws the water right down my back. Gordon's in the same state, barring the braid. I have to yell three times before he hears me.

"Gordie! Use General!" It takes a moment for him to see what I mean, then he lunges for the rope hanging from his saddle. In a minute he's lashed the rope around the log and the saddle horn.

"Pull, General!" Gordon's shouting his orders right by the horse's head, and I'm shouting them inside my own head as I try to guide the log. The water splashes and rushes past my shins.

The log jam blocks the creek. If we don't clear it soon, our little island will be flooded for sure, and we'll have a fast ride down the floodwaters to the Columbia, along with the Johansson's cows. If we can break up the jam, the creek will maybe stay in its bed and we can get out of the gully and ride home.

* * *

Gordon and I never should have been in the middle of this confounded creek on the side of a nameless mountain off the Conconully road. We should have been back on our neighboring farms in Omak, Washington, feeding the chickens and making sure the runoff from this rainstorm didn't channel the orchard or drown the chickens. But how could I stay home while everyone else was going to see some crazy man demonstrate his new flying machine, an aeroplane, at the fair up in Conconully? That's why I blame Daddy. He told us about it, then decided that, as the oldest, I would be the one who stayed home and took care of the place while he drove the rest of the family the twenty miles up the creek to see the aeroplane. He wouldn't have gone to the fair if I couldn't stay home, and I'd never have thought of going if he hadn't decided to go.

But how could I miss the only aeroplane I might ever see? Daddy said they were the future, and I'd see lots of them in my life, but I'm not so sure. Aeroplanes were so dangerous that until today, the only things I've heard of them doing is crashing. Maybe I kind of wanted to go to the fair because if the contraption was going to crash, I wanted to see it. Maybe this flood is a punishment for my horrible curiosity.

Mr. Russell, Gordon's father, would never go to a fair, so Gordon didn't think he'd ever see an aeroplane. We talked it over last night over chores.

"It's just not fair, that's all," I told him. "The twins get to go, but not me? Ruth and Barn are only seven! What do they know?"

"They're too young to stay home alone, is all." Gordon always tries to be calm and grown-up when I'm excited. It doesn't usually work. "You should be proud your Pa thinks you can handle all the chores," he told me.

I wish now I'd been satisfied with being seen as grown-up enough to take care of the farm alone. The boy's clothes I borrowed from Gordon are sopping wet and rubbing me raw in places I've never been rubbed, and we are likely to die right here.

But I didn't listen. Instead, I talked until Gordon listened to me. Anyway, we thought it was a lark. Mama and Daddy left before dawn with the wagon and the other kids. I thought David should have stayed home, because he's a boy, but Daddy said that nine is too young for that much responsibility. I'm thinking now that eleven is, too. Maybe if I'd been older, I'd have possessed the sense to do as I was told.

Maybe.

Gordon and I figured General could carry the two of us to Conconully in just a couple of hours, unlike Pet and Charlie with the wagon, which would take much of the day. We could do all our chores, ride up there in time to see the fair—especially the demonstration of the aeroplane—and ride back in time to do the evening chores. We might even get to enjoy the fair a bit. Daddy and the rest would drive home the next morning, so as long as we got back in time to do our evening chores, no one would be the wiser. I was sure it was a perfect plan.

The first half of the plan worked. We got away without being caught by Gordie's Pa, who wanted him to dig irrigation ditches, and we had a great time on the ride to Conconully. I borrowed a pair Gordie's overalls and a flannel shirt and put my hair under a hat so I'd look like a boy in case anyone saw us. The weather was nice, and we got to town in time to find a place where we could watch the show. I'd even brought a nickel to buy us a bite to eat, though we had to dodge once or twice when we saw people from Omak. Once we even saw Daddy. Good thing he's so tall I could spot im over the crowd. We hid under the stands to eat our ice cream and stayed to watch the air show.

The aeroplane looked awfully flimsy to me. I wouldn't go up in one, but Gordie would. He didn't say so, but I know by the way he watched every move that pile of wood and rags made. Watching set me breathing fast with excitement, but I was glad when the aviator landed safely. To my shock, someone announced that for two dollars he would take up passengers. Daddy makes two dollars in a whole day working with the horses at the big orchard down the river. So I knew none of my family would go up in that machine, and for once I was glad we were poor.

We had a good time, right up until we started home. Once we turned our back on the fair, we noticed the clouds that were building all day had turned as black as night. That worried us some, but not enough to take the edge off our fun. We were about halfway down the valley when it started to rain. Not just to rain—to *deluge.* That's one of my spelling words, and now I known what it means.

* * *

"Look out, Mattie!" Gordon rouses me from my thoughts again, and I jump aside just in time. The log shifts at last. I'm glad I thought of using General, because we'd never have moved it ourselves. The heavy log bucks and rolls and I run to General's head to keep him from spooking. Well, and because that looks like the safest place.

Once the log's out of the water, I hold General's bridle while Gordon unties the rope. Then we turn and watch the log jam. Even General and the cows watch, as though they, too, know how important this is.

"I think it's working," I say, as more water pushes through to run downstream. I don't think the water's climbing any higher up my legs. It's hard to tell because my pants couldn't get any wetter if the creek was up to my waist.

Gordon shakes his head. "The rest of the jam isn't budging. We have to move more logs."

I look at the water—deep, muddy, and fast—and at the mess of stuff that's blocking it. The only way to harness another log is for one of us to climb out there onto that dam. I swallow hard. I can't let Gordon know how scared I am.

"I think that one." I point at a many-branched log that might be holding the others in place. It's also near enough shore that maybe we can rope it without climbing onto the log jam.

He frowns. "I don't know."

"Look how it's holding all those other logs." I'm sure I'm right. "If we pull it out, the rest will either come along or wash downstream." I try not to remember that's what we said about the first log.

Gordon studies the log jam for so long I'm ready to scream with impatience. Doesn't he see how urgent this is? We have to act! But he's seeing something I can't, the way he does when we're building things and he knows just what to do next. I wait while Gordon stares into the flood. I watch the water creeping up toward us and fidget.

After an eternity he says, "That one," and points to a log farther out than the one I want. The water's piling up against it in its hurry to get downstream.

"That one? It's pretty far out." I try to sound like I'm just thinking the problem through, not like the idea of crawling across crashing and shifting logs scares the socks off me. Not that I'm wearing socks.

"I think it's the one."

I wish Gordon sounded more confident.

"It has to be from farther out this time," he says to convince us both. "The logs nearer shore are stuck on the bottom."

"But how will we drag that ashore with all the others in the way? Maybe we should just start at the edge and work our way out."

It's a sensible suggestion, and I can tell he knows it. But the rising water argues for a faster solution. Our little island is running out of space.

"We'll pull upstream," Gordon tells me. "Give me the rope."

I want to go out with him, but he won't let me. "Someone has to stay with General, or he'll panic. And if I go in—" he swallows hard, so I know he's almost as scared as I am. "If I go in, I'll hang onto the rope and maybe you can pull me out."

I don't point out what we both know. If he goes in the water amid that mess of logs, nothing on earth can save him.

"Promise if it's too bad you'll tie off to something else and we'll try doing it in bits," I insist. Gordon is busy checking where the rope is tied to the saddle horn and doesn't answer.

I stand at General's head, keeping him calm, and watch Gordon climb out onto the log jam. For a moment, I wonder if we couldn't climb all the way across to high ground, but I won't think about it. Even if we could cross, General and the cows couldn't. We are not going to let them die. The horse is a friend as well as awfully important to Gordon's family, and those cows probably mean the difference between success and starvation for the Johannsons.

Gordon is barefoot—we both have been all day, partly because we never wear shoes in summer, and partly because my shoes would give me away as a girl—and he moves across the near-shore logs almost at a run. Those are jammed into the mud enough to hold still while he climbs over them. As he moves farther out, I can see the logs shift and bounce under him. He stops trying to stand up and drops to his knees. Now he's crawling along, holding on with both hands, the end of the rope looped around his arm.

I concentrate all my thoughts on keeping him on the mess of bucking and bobbing logs, as if I can keep him safe by the force of my will.

After an eternity he reaches the log he picked out and ties the rope securely around one of the branches. I know it would be better if it were around the trunk, but there's no way for him to reach under water to loop it around. This will have to do. Gordon is on his way back, and I can almost start breathing again.

As soon as General feels the pull on the rope, he wants to start hauling. I have to stop watching

Gordon to keep General quiet. If we shift the log jam while Gordon's still out there—it doesn't bear thinking about, so I don't.

When I've calmed General and look up again, I can't see Gordon.

My heart stops. I'm sure it does. Then it's pounding so hard I can hardly breath. I look around wildly to find him. He must be ashore! But he's not.

He's gone.

He must have slipped off while I was busy with General, but I don't want to believe it.

If he's gone, I'm on my own. I still have to clear this jam. But if he's out there, if I just can't spot him, I don't dare move the logs.

I stand there for ages, staring at the log jam, hoping against hope.

Nothing.

I'm about to give General the command to pull, because the water's rising faster now, when I see an arm. It wraps around a branch that juts up out of the water, and in a moment, Gordon is back in view. I can't tell if he fell in or if he was just down on some lower part of the log jam where I couldn't see him. He's sopping wet, but we've both been sopping wet for ages, so that doesn't prove anything.

He's back on the solid part now, but he's still crawling over the logs, not up and moving fast like he did going out. I can see his mouth moving, but I can't hear him yelling.

He waves his arm in a signal to start pulling, but he's too far out, and moving too slowly. I wait until he's nearly ashore, even though the water is rising fast and General is tugging at the reins. General wants to get away from the shifting weight against the saddle horn. At last I think Gordon's close enough in to be safe.

"Hi-yah!" I slap General with the reins and lead

him forward. He bends to the effort, and I divide my attention between him and the log jam. Our rope pulls up out of the water, draws tight, and we stop. General digs in his hooves, lowers his head, and pulls harder.

I hold my breath. *Dear God, don't let the rope break!* It's all I can think while I watch General strain.

*Where's Gordon?* I look around in a hurry and see that he's safe, but he's sitting down, too close to the water. Maybe too close to the log jam to be safe when it comes loose. He must be too tired to move, but I can't stop now. I lean in and whisper to General every loving and encouraging word I can think of.

The log shifts.

It's almost nothing at first, but then I see it move, and General takes a step forward. Then another. The end of the log pulls out of the tangle, dragging a snarl of smaller branches and mess with it. A big glob of sagebrush and sticks and who knows what else moves, and I finally see what Gordon planned. The log pulls loose and leaves a gap in the dam.

Gordon looks up and cheers, and so do I. It's working. The opening we created allows the water to flow through faster, and the log jam is breaking up.

Suddenly Gordon's shouts change. General digs in, but he's pulled back a step. His head comes up and he snorts in fear.

"Cut the rope!" Gordon yells. Why doesn't he come do it? I don't have a knife in my pocket. I'm not a boy.

"There's a knife on the saddle!"

Of course. I struggle to reach the sheath without dropping the reins. What will General do when the rope lets go?

"Give him his head!" Gordon's still shouting instructions. "Cut the rope at the horn! And stand clear!"

*Oh, Lord!* It's a prayer, the way the words come into my mind. I drop the reins and manage to reach the knife. Unlike any pocketknife I've ever owned, Gordon's sheath knife is sharp. One slash and the rope is gone. I only just manage to duck in time to avoid it whipping my face as the end flies free. I jump back farther to avoid General's dancing hooves. The sudden release from the pull almost knocks him to his knees. Surely by now, Gordon will be here to help me. But he isn't.

I have to take care of General. I'm scared of those big hooves, but General's more scared, and it's up to me. I lunge for the reins, and on the third try I get them.

"Whoa, easy boy." I don't know if he can hear me over the noise of the creek, which roars louder now that the water is moving again. I pull down, hard. Maybe he can feel me through the reins, or maybe he's just had time to figure out what happened. He calms down, and I pull his head to me to comfort him with an arm around his neck.

Finally, I have time to look around for Gordon. He's still sitting in the mud, but farther from the water than he was. Only on a second look do I realize that he hasn't moved. The water that threatened to overwhelm us really is dropping. Our island is safe, for the time being.

I raise my arms and cheer, but Gordon still doesn't come join me. I want to hold his hands and dance around in my happiness at not dying here, but he isn't even looking at me.

When I really look at him, I notice his head's down on his knees and he's holding his leg.

I lead General to him at a run.

"Gordie! You're hurt." I'm not even sure he's conscious.

After a minute he looks up. His face is dead white under the muddy smears. "I've hurt my foot. Bad," he adds.

He's right. I can see his foot is already turning colors. To my frightened eyes, it looks about twice the size it should be. Now I know why he didn't come help me. He can't walk.

"What happened?" I know it must have happened while I wasn't watching. Is it my fault, for not keeping him safe with my eyes?

"I slipped. My foot got stuck. I thought I was a goner, but I got it out. I think it's broken, though."

I don't tell him I thought he was gone and almost pulled the log jam loose from under him.

"Can you get on General?" I ask instead. He needs a doctor, and we have to get out of here before fresh floodwaters come down on us. If we can.

"I think I can. If you help me." He moves to stand.

"Wait." I don't know if it will help, but I take both of our big bandana handkerchiefs—I'm glad I borrowed one to go along with the overalls—and tie his foot up. Gordon says a bad word when I do.

"Is it too tight?"

"No." He grits out the word, so I know it must really hurt. I can't tell if he's crying, because the rain is still running down our faces. "It has to be tight."

I pull him up, and he leans on my shoulder. He can't put any weight on the foot.

"Come here, General," he commands, and the horse moves closer. "You'll need both hands to help me up. General will stand, won't you, boy?"

I'm not so sure. General is a good horse, but he's had a trying day.

"How do we get you up there?" General has never seemed so tall before.

Gordon studies the problem. It's his way. Never hurry, think it through. I wish I were as good at that, but I'm impatient.

"I can boost you if you put your knee on my back, I think."

Gordon's bigger than I am. I'm not at all sure I can hold his weight, but I'll do whatever I must to get us out of this. He nods agreement to my plan. Then he lets go of my shoulder and grabs the saddle with both hands, holding himself up. I squat down, and he puts his knee on my back, his injured foot sticking out behind us. I brace myself as I take the weight. He's holding as much of his weight as he can with the saddle horn. "Okay. One, two, *three!*"

On *three* he lunges upward, and I straighten my knees to raise him more, glad for once of all the times I've climbed to the top end of the orchard or down to the river for water. My legs are strong and push him upwards.

Now Gordon's lying across the saddle on his stomach. General shifts uneasily and, seeing Gordon is holding himself there, I take up the reins again.

"Easy, General. Hold still."

The horse gives me a look as if to say, "I've had about enough of this," but he stands while Gordon shifts himself about until he's astride.

"Now to get me up there," I say. I've just realized that he's always boosted me up. I'm not tall enough to get a foot into the stirrup and swing up the way he does when both his feet work. I look around for something to climb on, but there's nothing.

"Maybe I can pull you up?"

We try, but I keep slipping back down. I don't want to pull him off, so we give up.

I'm in a hurry to move. There's a rushing stream behind us and only a shallow trickle ahead, where there should be no stream at all. I watch it with one eye, waiting for the water to come flooding back like the roaring monster it is.

I wrap the reins around my hand and start walking. Gordon settles into the saddle, hanging onto the horn. He looks like he might pass out at any minute. I have to get us out of the stream bed.

The water's a little deeper than I thought, but it's no longer fast and deep enough to push me off my feet. I hang on tight to the reins just in case. If I lose my footing, General will drag me out. He won't like it, though. I'm careful and cross without any trouble.

The scramble up the steep side of the gully nearly unseats Gordon, but he hangs on with a determination that matches the pain he must be feeling. When the ground levels out, I stop.

I've forgotten about the cattle. Do I need to go back and drive them off the island? Gordon needs me, but if we don't save the cattle, it was all a waste.

To my relief, the cows have followed us on their own. The leaders are bucking and snorting their way up the bank. From here they can find their way home. I bet they are as cured of running off as I am.

Again, I look for a mounting block. A rock does the job, and I manage to squirm into the saddle in front of Gordon. We don't even discuss it. We both know he can't handle the reins and manage General. I just hope he won't fall off.

We both shiver with cold, or maybe reaction, but Gordon is shaking worse than I am. He wraps an arm through my suspenders to keep himself upright, and I kick General into a walk with my muddy bare heels. I'm in a hurry, but I don't want Gordon to fall off. Or me. I'm not that good a rider, and I'm too short to reach the stirrups.

If Gordon weren't hurt, I'd suggest we hide out for a while. We'll be home before Mama and Daddy get back from the fair, but it's hours past chore-time, nearing dark. Gordon's Pa will be tan-your-hide angry, and I know I won't escape just because I'm not his kid.

Gordon says what I'm thinking. "We are in so much trouble, Mattie. If it weren't for this darned foot, I'd say let's run off to Seattle and go to sea."

I laugh. It feels good after being tensed up for so long. "I guess so! But you need a doctor. Maybe they'll be so worried about that they'll forget to punish us."

Gordie laughs, too, a good sound. I can hear the pain though. He shifts. I think he's turning to look back. His words confirm that. "The cows are still following us. Saving those cows might save our hides. Pa knows any man would do whatever he had to so's he could save a neighbor's herd."

After that we ride in silence. In a few minutes we can see Gordon's farm, with our orchard next to it. My house is hidden behind the trees. If this had worked the way it was supposed to, I'd slide off General when we reached the edge of the orchard, and Gordon would ride in like he'd just been out to clear the irrigation ditch or something. I'd do my chores and no one would be the wiser.

I don't even mention that plan. I point General at Gordon's house. When we get there, we have another problem. He can't get down alone, and I'm not strong enough to hold him. I can't even get down from the saddle myself, because he's holding on to me now like his life depends on it.

"Let go!" I say.

Gordon doesn't answer. I crane my head around to look at him and start yelling.

Gordon has fainted.

* * *

In the confusion while everyone fusses over him, I slip away. He can tell whatever story he wants when he's able to speak. It's not that I'm trying to get out of the punishment we've both earned. Well, not entirely. I won't mind putting that off, and I need to do my chores. I walk back through the orchard. The sun's gone down. What with the rain and the clouds it's extra dark, but I know the way.

I've been shivering for an hour. I can't wait to get warm and dry.

When I get there, the chickens are setting up a mighty fuss, the cow is bellowing her need to be milked, and the fire in the kitchen stove is dead out. I just want to lie down and sleep, but the animals need me. I skin out of Gordon's wet overalls and into my own dry dress and run for the barn. I hurry to get the cow in, telling her how sorry I am to be late.

While I milk, I remember the little aeroplane sailing through the skies over Conconully. What happened afterwards tries to push in, but I make myself keep seeing the smooth fabric wings against the sun instead of the crashing logs that almost crushed my friend.

Maybe someday I will fly after all.

It can't be worse than this afternoon.

The End

Rebecca M. Douglass is a writer of children's fiction, cozy mysteries, and fantasy. When not writing, she likes to spend her time hiking, biking, and traveling with her husband. She works at the local library, where she hopes to learn the secrets of the Ninja Librarian.
www.ninjalibrarian.com
www.facebook.com/RebeccaDouglassNinjaLibrarian

# Winter Days
## By Katharina Gerlach

"Tim? Katie? We're getting close to the border. Remember, no talking! Even if they ask you something, you're not to speak," Father reminded us as we sped along the tarmac. Trees stood on either side of the road, flitting past so fast they blurred into each other. The melting snow made the whole countryside look gray and forlorn, and the air coming through the air vents smelled of snow and wet soil.

"Pah," Tim said. "I'm not afraid of some border patrol guards." My brother, only eleven months younger than I, liked to pretend he knew everything, but he didn't. Maybe he needed to grow as old as me to understand how dangerous this journey was.

"We will all end up in prison," Mother said in a shaky voice that scared me more than father's threat to burn all our toys if we talked at the border. Tim snorted and folded his arms in front of his chest. His bright red jumper crumpled as he stared at his jeans with a deep crease on his forehead. I buried my face in the book I'd taken along to pass the time. It was a long journey.

A tiny house made of red bricks with an equally red roof stood in the middle of the road like a toll booth. Two border guards dressed in dark green uniforms stood inside. Father slowed the car and stopped while Mother fished our passports from the handbag she'd clutched for the last half hour.

Suddenly my heart thumped in my throat. I pressed my lips together, watching one of the green men study the documents.

"You could have gone six years ago," he said to

148

my father.

"Didn't trust them."

"So why now?" The border guard handed back the passports.

Father shrugged. "A friend of mine encouraged me. He said he never had any trouble going."

"And anyway, it's Christmas," Mother added. Her smile looked a little wobbly on her face, as if it didn't belong.

"Have a good time." The border guard stepped back into his little hut and waved us along.

"See, that wasn't so bad," Tim said as Father accelerated.

"That was the West German border guard." My father's voice sounded like the time Tim had fallen off a ladder and everyone thought him dead. "The others will be..." He didn't finish his sentence. A concrete tower came into view—square, gray, and with a machine gun in the windowless room at the top that pointed at the road. Father slowed the car to a crawl.

"Do we have to go so slow?" Tim shifted in his seat and stared at the barbed wire fence that stretched out to either side of the road. I could tell he was getting nervous, too. So, I wiped one of my sweaty hands on my jumper and squeezed Tim's hand. He didn't pull back, which confirmed his fear.

Mother pointed to a street sign, a red bordered white circle with a black thirty in the middle, and then to the watchtower that now loomed nearly overhead. Tim slipped closer to me.

We drove along the road for a good, long while, but the ice in my stomach never melted. The road widened into seven, eight, or more lanes. A young man in a gray uniform waved us into the second lane toward some waiting cars. I wondered why we couldn't use one of the empty lanes but didn't dare ask.

Father stopped the car behind three vehicles just

as the first one moved into a gigantic hall covered with a roof. The whole setup resembled a very big fuel station, but instead of pumps, small gray houses sat between the lanes. The car that had been motioned to enter stopped and all its passengers stepped out of the vehicle. They took their suitcases and followed another gray guard into one of the houses. At once several grays moved around the car. Too many crowded around to see what they were doing, but they had a long rod and a handle attached to a nearly horizontal mirror on wheels, so they were up to something.

Then, the wait began. Tim grew fidgety, but whenever he opened his mouth to ask one of his endless questions, I put a finger to my lips and jerked my head toward the gray clad guards. They scared me even worse than the silence of my parents.

A car approached on the far lane, slowed, stopped, and was waved on by the guards. I wondered about that, and knew Tim would too, but before he could ask his inevitable questions, Father explained. "That's the transit route to Berlin. Since the people in that car won't enter the German Democratic Republik, they don't have to be searched."

The car in front of us shifted forward, and so he started the motor again and moved up to a white line on the road. Another gray guard stood there, holding out his hand. Father cranked down the window while Mother held out our passports again.

"Where to?" The guard practically ripped the documents from mother's hand. I flinched at the ice in his voice and because the cold air sliced through the comfortable warmth of the car's interior.

"Feldberg, Brandenburg." Father snapped out the words, not adding an explanation or greeting or anything else.

"Are those your children?" The guard bent down and stared into the back of the car. I'd never in my life seen brown eyes that looked so cold. I froze like a drop of water in winter and barely dared to breathe. Tim stiffened, too, and his hand squeezed mine harder. Even if we had wanted to, we couldn't have uttered a word.

The guard straightened and went back to studying the passports, only glancing at my mother. Then, his eyes bored into my father's. "Well, well. Republikflüchtling, eh?"

In the rear view mirror, I saw my father's face harden. The word must mean something really, really bad—like murder. But I just knew my father had never killed a man. They must be mistaken.

"Pre seventy-two," he said. His voice was pressed. My heart dropped and I stiffened as if my whole body had turned to ice. My father—my strong, invincible father—was clearly afraid. Was my heart even still beating?

The guard took a step backward without returning the documents. He pointed to the next lane over in the gigantic hall. "Park there and step out of the car."

Pale as death, Father complied. When he and Mother helped us out of the car, their hands trembled enough for me to notice. I wanted nothing more than to run home, but my body moved only sluggishly. Even the icy air seemed warmer than the border guards. We lined up beside one of the doors of the little gray houses and waited. I tried not to breathe too deeply since the air stank of exhaust fumes.

In moments, a bunch of grays surrounded our car. They used a long, bendy metal rod to poke into our fuel tank and pushed a little mirror on wheels under our car. Someone measured widths and heights of the interior with a tape measure. Tim's mouth opened and closed, a telltale sign for his rising curiosity. I grabbed his hand again to remind him to be silent and willed him to remember. Father had explained before the journey they would be looking for smuggling compartments. Since we had none, we would be fine. But the cold glances of the grays didn't reassure me one bit.

"Fetch your suitcases and come with me," a female voice beside me said. I spun around and stared at a stocky woman in a gray dress that went down to her knees. Somehow it reassured me a little to see the gooseflesh on her bare legs. It indicated that she wasn't all that different from us. I wouldn't have been able to follow her order otherwise.

I picked up my backpack with the books and the toys I'd decided to bring and followed my family into a room. The woman asked us to put our suitcase and the backpacks on a big table and step back. Leaning against the wall, we watched in silence as the woman turned our suitcase inside out. She took everything out, emptied both backpacks, and left everything in an untidy pile.

A man entered and told my father to follow him. As I watched them leave, my knees wobbled so hard, I could barely stand, and a giant fist squeezed my heart. Would I ever see him again?

"Spread your arms and legs wide," the woman said to Mother, and my mother complied. Beads of sweat covered her forehead, and I thought I heard her heart thunder. But it was only my own.

The woman patted Mother down, then waved her to the table. "You can re-pack your suitcase." She turned to Tim and me and crouched. There was a gentleness in her eyes I hadn't expected. "Don't worry, dears," she said. "I only need to make sure you're not carrying anything illegal into the GDR." Carefully—as if we were made of porcelain—she patted me and then Tim down, too. "There, that didn't hurt, did it?" She even smiled.

Still, Tim hid his face in my teddy bear the minute

we got our toys back. I could have used the bear myself but decided not to fight about it. Tim was so much younger, he probably needed it more.

You can't imagine my relief when Father returned just as Mother closed the suitcase. Without a word, he picked it up and carried it back to the car where the flock of gray border guards had vanished. We entered and waited. Only when yet another guard waved us forward did Father start the engine and drove the few meters forward.

The man handed us back out passports. "Remember that you've got to report to Feldberg police station by tomorrow morning latest," he said. "You'll need your letter of admission, the passports, and the receipt for the money exchange."

Father just nodded. The guard pointed out of the hall toward a tiny, ugly, gray, flat roofed house. "You can use the exchange station here." Then, he waved us on.

As instructed, Father left the car at the money exchange station, entered the building, and returned with a wad of bills and coins. The coins were made of alloy. Holding them felt like holding no money at all, they were so light.

Mother put the money into her purse, and Father snorted. "Thirteen West Mark a day for every person except the children. That must be the most expensive zoo in the world." It was meant as a joke, but no one laughed.

As we drove on, I expected to feel relieved, but I didn't. There were still watch towers with guns trained on our car, still barbed wire fences, still long stretches of land without any sign of habitation. At last, we passed a white and red striped bar that could be used to block the road but that stood open at the moment. Another tiny hut with a gray border guard stood beside it. He paid us no heed.

Once past that, Father said. "That was that. You may now speak again, kids."

I was too shaken from the experience, but Tim had thousands of questions. "Why do they point guns at the cars? Is the piece of fence standing off from the main fence at an angle there to keep people from crossing the border? But why is it pointing toward the GDR? Why did they search all out luggage? Why... why... why..."

I tuned him out and watched the streets where slowly more cars showed up. The scent of the air coming through the vents changed to an ugly mix of snow, exhaust fumes, and the sweet-ashy odor of burnt coal. Most cars looked like cardboard boxes on wheels, some gray, some beige, and some baby blue. The villages and towns we passed were gray, too; gray walls with holes in the plaster, gray tarmac and cobble stone roads with gray snow sludge in the gutters, gray roofs, gray front gardens—even the trees and the people seemed gray. I asked my parents if gray was the GDR's national color.

Mother shook her head. "It's just difficult to get supplies and tools for renovations. Also, everything looks grayer in winter than usual anyway."

Hours later—Tim had fallen asleep—we entered yet another one of the gray cities. It was already late afternoon and the sun lost the fight against the sky's cloud cover.

"I think we'd better get it over and done with," Father said. "Then we can think about Christmas again."

Mother agreed, and so we parked our car and walked up a steep, cobble stone road to the town's police station. When Father explained at the information desk why we had come, the clerk pointed us to a corridor with many doors. The walls were painted a weak green, and the air smelled of cleaning detergents. We sat on a row of uncomfortable brown wooden chairs and waited for the door in front of us to open. Tim fell asleep again on Mother's lap.

And then, everything went very fast. We were ushered into a room just as green as the corridor. Mother still carried Tim who buried his head against her shoulder. Another woman in gray sat at a wooden desk. She didn't look up from the papers in front of her and didn't greet us either. Pen poised, she asked, "You arrived today?"

"Yes," Father said and laid the passports, a letter, and the receipt of the money exchange onto the table. "We'll be staying with my best friend and his family." He gave her the address, and she nodded.

"How long are you going to stay?" Finally, she looked up. I wasn't surprised to see that her eyes were gray too. Maybe everyone in this country turned gray eventually.

"Second of January." Mother's voice sounded firm and warm as she set Tim down. My brother clung to her like a toddler. I relaxed a little, leaning against her other side.

"Make sure you're on time," the woman said. "We're not looking gently at Republikflüchtlinge that are late."

"Naturally." Father bowed his head slightly.

"Due to year-end holidays, you'll have to check out on December 28th." She handed Father a slip of paper, and soon after we walked back to our car. It was telling that Tim didn't dare ask a question until we drove out of town.

"What is a Republikflüchtling?" he wanted to know. He'd woken enough to be his old eager self.

"When I was a young man, Germany was divided into four zones. We'd lost the war, and so the four parties that won split up the country," Father explained while we drove the final half hour to his best friend's house. "The parts that are now West Germany eventually got their independence back, but the part that's now GDR, the part where I used to live, remained under Soviet supervision.

"You know that I always wanted to become a forester and nothing else? Well, since I always spoke my mind, my marks were really bad and eventually I got kicked out of school for a critical essay I wrote. The only way to become a forester was a school in West Germany, and so I left the GDR just before they built the German-German border. The government here considers that a major crime they call Flight from the Republic, or Republikflucht. They only pardoned people who fled before seventy-two a few years ago."

"So they know you!" I had a lightbulb moment.

"They surely have a file on me, yes."

Mother threw Tim a stern look. "Therefore, we need to make sure not to offend them in any way until we're out of the country again, or we will all end up in prison."

A shiver rolled down my spine nearly as cold as the air outside.

\* \* \*

Our destination was the house of a forester in a village of maybe ten houses and a shop in the center. There were potholes in the cobble stone road deep enough to become small lakes when it rained. Father drove around them to prevent damage to the car.

But his best friend's house was a positive surprise. Green garlands hung everywhere, and the family wore colorful clothes. From the car we stepped into a world separate from the rest of what I'd seen of the GDR.

The next days passed in a flurry of activities. Christmas presents had to be sorted and food cooked. We searched and found a fir tree in the forest, cut it, took it home, and decorated it.

My father's best friend had a family with children

156

too, and we hit it off immediately. We roamed through the forest, discovering whatever there was to discover, building forts, pretending to fight, and generally having a good time. Christmas came and went, and soon the time for our departure neared.

"I'm going into town to get us checked out with the police," Father said to Mother. We were sitting at the huge, wooden breakfast table with the checkered cloth and enough room to feed an army.

Naturally we escaped parental supervision as soon as we could. Outside, we played Zorro, with me as the vigilante's girlfriend—which I hated; I rather wanted to be Zorro, but that honor went to the eldest of us. I waved as Father drove off. For a moment, I worried he wouldn't come back, but then play took over and time flew. I never noticed his return until I saw our car parked in the driveway. An ice ball in my stomach melted I hadn't known existed.

Soon after lunch, the rain set in, and we were called inside. Luckily the house had a gigantic tiled stove fed from the hall but extending through all the downstairs rooms. In the living room, it ended three or four feet below the ceiling, leaving a bed wide enough for us children. So, we withdrew there to play.

"The rain has turned to snow." Mother came in with her arms full of carrots from the garden shed for tonight's salad. We children ran outside as fast as we could put on our coats. In a flurry of arms and legs, we tried to catch the snowflakes, laughing more than actually catching one. I was the best at that. The trick was to hold your breath as you stuck out your tongue or the snowflake would melt before its delicious iciness reached your tongue.

The snowfall intensified and even the toddler managed to catch a flake or two. When Mother called us in for dinner, little snowdrifts already formed at the lee side of the sheds.

I woke in the middle of the night when Tim crawled into my bed.

"It's so cold," he whispered. His breath condensed and rained down on us in little ice crystals.

"Maybe we should wake Mother," I suggested just as the door to our bedroom opened and Dorie, the wife of Father's best friend, came in with a candle.

"The electricity failed which also means no central heating," she said. "Come downstairs to the living room, children. Everybody is already there, and we've heated up the tiled stove."

Downstairs, we huddled as close to the stove as we could while Dorie and Mother filled crooked apples with raisins and sprinkled them with sugar and cinnamon. The apples went into the oven part of the tiled stove, and we played card games, wondering when the electricity would be restored.

It turned out the snowfall developed into a blizzard, dumping piles of snow onto the world. Out of the windows, we could see snow drifts higher than I was tall. It was all a big adventure. We spent the rest of the night on the wonderfully warm bed on top of the tiled stove, talking and eating baked apples and feeling cozy and happy. After all, we were together.

But days passed and the snow didn't go away. The phone line had died too, so we couldn't even call anyone to ask for advice. Father suspected one of the overland poles had fallen due to the snow.

My Mother grew more and more unsettled as the second of January drew near. "When will the snowplows come?" she'd ask, but everyone just shook their heads. No one knew.

When New Year passed without celebration, I finally realized what being snowed in meant.

"Remember the gray lady at the police station?" I said to Tim, and he nodded.

"They'll lock us up for good if we don't make it out

of the GDR before tomorrow night." His face was as pale as the snow behind the window. "What can we do?"

I bent forward and whispered into his ear. "We need to fetch someone with a snowplow big enough to clear the road."

Tim swallowed but nodded. "Tonight," he whispered back.

"It's only a kilometer or two to the village." We'd walked to the small shop in the village's center that people here called Konsum on the first day we arrived, so I knew it wouldn't take all that long. Still, I had to encourage us both since walking through a snow filled night alone seemed pretty scary. "One of the farmers is bound to have a snowplow."

"We'd better wear our snow trousers," Tim said, but then one of the other children asked what we were doing and soon we were engaged in play again.

\* \* \*

That night, the other children and I huddled together on top of the tiled stove, and the grown-ups drug mattresses as close to it as possible. They even went to bed at the same time as we did. Everyone lay buried under several blankets. Soon the children beside me relaxed into sleep. Tim even snored a little, but I couldn't sleep. Listening to the howling wind outside, I watched the glowing world behind the windows. The moon was but a sliver of silver on a star-studded sky, but the snow reflected its light, brightening the night. At least we wouldn't need a lantern.

Below me, the adults whispered quietly.

"What if the snowplow won't come tomorrow morning?" The worry in Mother's voice shook me. I pulled my blanket closer.

"Well, they can't put you in jail if they're responsible for uncleared roads," Dorie said. "After all, you can't make your car fly over the snowbanks."

"I'm a Republikflüchtling." Father's voice held as much dread as Mother's, which chilled me as if I'd spent the day outdoors. "I'm not sure the same rules apply for me as they do for others."

They kept whispering for a while longer but didn't find a solution for the problem. The only option was to wait for a snowplow. My determination to walk into the village to fetch someone intensified. I barely could wait for the grown-ups to fall asleep, too.

When I was sure that everyone slept, I nudged my bother. He groaned and rolled over. I shook him to no avail. Finally, I slipped off the tiled stove on my own. I fetched my clothes, went into the hall, and dressed there. I put on every bit of warm clothing I could find in the dark, including two scarves and Father's gloves over mine. Then, I slipped out of the back door.

Father and his best friend had cleared paths around the cars, to the sheds, and to the street, and the snow they'd shoveled away towered beside me, blocking out what little light the moon provided. They'd even cleared a little bit of the road but not as thoroughly as the paths through their yard. The air smelled fresh as if the snow had washed it clean. Determination coursed through my veins and so I turned left and walked toward the village.

With every step, I sank deeper into the snow. After but a few yards, I had to fight my way out of snowdrifts every single step of the way, only to crash through the thin layer of ice on the next one. I grew hot in the layers of my winter clothing, which made the snow melt. Ice water seeped in at the openings for arms, legs, and neck, mingling with my sweat and soaking me in no time.

I grew cold, most of all my nose. Moving forward was exhausting and I wished I could simply turn around and go back. The tip of my nose hurt, I was cold and miserable, and I shivered despite sweating profusely. But I made my way forward, step by step and inch by inch.

I kept telling myself that it wasn't far to the village, and that was true—not on a snow free day. I soon realized that in this kind of snow, it might as well be on another planet. I tried to turn around to walk back, but by now the moon had set and I could no longer find my own trail.

I called for help. "Mother!" I was so tired I could barely lift my legs anymore. "Father!"

Were those flowers blooming along the way? Why was it so warm all of a sudden? And why did the air carry the scent of freshly mowed grass and the fragrance of roses? Hadn't I been in the middle of a snow-filled night just now? This couldn't be real. My eyelids were so heavy they kept drooping, and the tip of my nose hurt. When I touched it, pain shot through me and the world around me came back into focus. Yes, everything was snow as far as I could see.

"There!"

A voice. I must be near the village. I struggled out of the snowdrift once more to take the next step.

Warm arms encircled me and lifted me up. Father had come. Tears filled my eyes. Everything would be good now. We'd get a plow and return home and the grays wouldn't have any reason to put us in prison. With a sigh I sank against his chest.

When I opened my eyes next, I rested naked on Mother's lap, wrapped in blankets and surrounded by hot water bottles. Tim kept glancing at me with guilt written all over his face. So, he'd told them about my plan. But I didn't have the energy to be angry, and if I thought about it—which was a lot more difficult than usual—he'd saved my life with his babbling. How far had I come?

"Did we get a snowplow?" Why was my voice so

hoarse?

"Oh honey!" Mother hugged me so hard, I struggled to breathe. "Don't ever do that again. Promise! I'd rather be in prison *with* you than back home *without* you."

Those were the last words I heard before I drifted off to sleep again.

* * *

It turned out that I hadn't even made it past the far end of the garden fence, a mere two hundred meters or so in the direction of the village. At least the energy came back the day after my failed try, but we had to wait another three days before a snowplow finally rumbled past the house.

We left early the next morning, promising to visit again sometime soon if we didn't end up in prison.

The drive was uneventful but slow since the roads were still partially covered with snow and sludge. We arrived at the border way after dark and stopped at the end of a very, very long row of cars. It seemed more families than just us were caught by the snow.

It took forever to get to the gray clad guards. My heart clenched, and my stomach twisted. My hands and feet were as cold as during that night, but I still noted that the guard looked rather tired.

"You're three days late," he said as he took the passports from Father.

"The snowplow didn't come." It was our only excuse, and I shivered with fear. I didn't want to go to prison.

"You're a Republikflüchtling, right?"

"Pre seventy-two." Father answered the same as the last time.

The silence stretched as the guard studied the passports. I felt like vomiting. Any second now, we'd be arrested and taken to prison. And only because I didn't make it into the village. So, I did the only thing

I could think of, despite my promise not to speak.

"I really tried to get a plow," I said and pointed to the chilblain on my nose. "See? This is proof."

Mother blushed and Father explained to the guard what had happened.

And then, something happened I never, ever expected. A smile grew on the guard's face. It was as if the sun rose and melted his iciness.

"Quite the hero, eh?" He handed back the passports. "Have a good journey."

As we drove away into the most glorious winter a child could dream of, I realized that the Eastern German border guards, under all their grayness, were as human as we were. And that they, too, waited for the spring.

The End


A studied forester and mother of three, bilingual Katharina Gerlach has been making up tales like forever. Since practice makes perfect-ish, she's now writing daily, mostly fantasy and historical stories in English and German. In December, she runs the annual online Indie Authors' Advent Calendar with daily flash fiction stories.
www.katharinagerlach.com
www.facebook.com/KatharinaGerlach.Autorin
www.twitter.com/CatGerlach

**A Writer's Digest 101 Best Websites for Writers and The Write Life's 100 Best Websites for Writers**

The Insecure Writer's Support Group was founded by science fiction author Alex J. Cavanaugh in September of 2011. Its purpose—to encourage, support, and inform. The website is a database resource for writers and authors, with weekly guests and tips, thousands of links, and a monthly newsletter. There is also an annual Twitter pitch (#IWSGPit), a monthly bloghop the first Wednesday of every month, a Facebook and Instagram group, and @TheIWSG on Twitter.

Website: www.insecurewriterssupportgroup.com/
Facebook: www.facebook.com/groups/IWSG13/
Twitter: www.twitter.com/TheIWSG/
Instagram: www.instagram.com/theiwsg/
Email: admin@insecurewriterssupportgroup.com
Newsletter signup: www.
insecurewriterssupportgroup.us12.list-manage.
com/subscribe?u=b058c62fa7ffb4280355e8854&id=
cc6abce571

OTHER BOOKS:

**Masquerade: Oddly Suited**
Find love at the ball...
Print ISBN 9781939844644
EBook ISBN 9781939844651

**Tick Tock: A Stitch in Crime**
The clock is ticking...
Print ISBN 9781939844545

EBook ISBN 9781939844552

**Mysteries of Death and Life**
Can a lost hero find redemption?
Print ISBN 9781939844361
EBook ISBN 9781939844378

**Parallels: Felix Was Here**
Enter the realm of parallel universes!
Print ISBN 9781939844194
EBook ISBN 9781939844200

FREE BOOKS:

**The Insecure Writer's Support Group Writing for Profit**
EBook ISBN: 9781939844453

**The Insecure Writer's Support Group Guide to Publishing and Beyond**
EBook ISBN 9781939844088

CPSIA information can be obtained
at www.ICGtesting.com
Printed in the USA
FSHW011322070420
68909FS